She Was Not Going To Fall For Garrett Holden.

He was a bully and a brute and a mean, hateful person…but that hadn't been true for the five days since what she'd come to think of as The Television Truce. And if he smiled at her one more time, and spoke to her in that deep, dark, honey-over-whiskey voice, she might just grab him by the hair and kiss him until this ridiculous fascination was slaked.

She was *not* going to fall for him.

She didn't feel that way about Garrett.

Yet.

Dear Reader,

Looking for romances with a healthy dose of passion? Don't miss Silhouette Desire's red-hot May lineup of passionate, powerful and provocative love stories!

Start with our MAN OF THE MONTH, *His Majesty, M.D.*, by bestselling author Leanne Banks. This latest title in the ROYAL DUMONTS miniseries features an explosive engagement of convenience between a reluctant royal and a determined heiress. Then, in Kate Little's *Plain Jane & Doctor Dad,* the new installment of Desire's continuity series DYNASTIES: THE CONNELLYS, a rugged Connelly sweeps a pregnant heroine off her feet.

A brooding cowboy learns about love and family in *Taming Blackhawk,* a SECRETS! title by Barbara McCauley. Reader favorite Sara Orwig offers a brand-new title in the exciting TEXAS CATTLEMAN'S CLUB: THE LAST BACHELOR series. In *The Playboy Meets His Match,* enemies become lovers and then some.

A sexy single mom is partnered with a lonesome rancher in Kathie DeNosky's *Cassie's Cowboy Daddy.* And in Anne Marie Winston's *Billionaire Bachelors: Garrett,* sparks fly when a tycoon shares a cabin with the woman he believes was his stepfather's mistress.

Bring passion into your life this month by indulging in all six of these sensual sizzlers.

Enjoy!

Joan Marlow Golan

Joan Marlow Golan
Senior Editor, Silhouette Desire

Please address questions and book requests to:
Silhouette Reader Service
U.S.: 3010 Walden Ave., P.O. Box 1325, Buffalo, NY 14269
Canadian: P.O. Box 609, Fort Erie, Ont. L2A 5X3

Billionaire Bachelors: Garrett

ANNE MARIE WINSTON

Silhouette

Desire

Published by Silhouette Books

America's Publisher of Contemporary Romance

SILHOUETTE BOOKS

ISBN 0-373-76440-5

BILLIONAIRE BACHELORS: GARRETT

Books by Anne Marie Winston

Silhouette Desire

Best Kept Secrets #742
Island Baby #770
Chance at a Lifetime #809
Unlikely Eden #827
Carolina on My Mind #845
Substitute Wife #863
Find Her, Keep Her #887
Rancher's Wife #936
Rancher's Baby #1031
Seducing the Proper Miss Miller #1155
*The Baby Consultant #1191
*Dedicated to Deirdre #1197
*The Bride Means Business #1204
Lovers' Reunion #1226
The Pregnant Princess #1268
Seduction, Cowboy Style #1287
Rancher's Proposition #1322
Tall, Dark & Western #1339
A Most Desirable M.D. #1371
Risqué Business #1407
Billionaire Bachelors: Ryan #1413
Billionaire Bachelors: Stone #1423
Billionaire Bachelors: Garrett #1440

*Butler County Brides

ANNE MARIE WINSTON

RITA® Award finalist and bestselling author Anne Marie Winston loves babies she can give back when they cry, animals in all shapes and sizes, and just about anything that blooms. When she's not writing, she's chauffeuring children to various activities, trying *not* to eat chocolate or reading anything she can find. She will dance at the slightest provocation and weeds her gardens when she can't see the sun for the weeds anymore. You can learn more about Anne Marie's novels by visiting her Web site at www.annemariewinston.com.

For Lucie and Missy, the original roadkill kitties,
and for the staff of the Waynesboro Veterinary Clinic.
For many years of excellent care and for services
above and beyond the call of sanity!

One

Garrett Holden strode up the cracking sidewalk and stepped onto the low front porch of the dilapidated half-house. He shook his head in disgust as he looked around the tiny dwelling. This was what he got for insisting that he be the one to notify the woman mentioned in his stepfather Robin Underwood's will of Robin's death.

This wasn't an area of Baltimore he usually frequented, with its tiny, narrow duplexes all crammed together on the streets across from the far reaches of the Johns Hopkins University campus. The front yards were minuscule. The backs, as he'd discovered when he'd driven down the alley behind the house on his initial pass, consisted largely of concrete slabs, not a blade of grass in sight. He'd been relieved to find a parking space within sight of the address where he could keep an eye on his imported sports car. Though he hadn't seen anyone suspicious, the area looked like a prime target for crime. He couldn't imagine how on earth Robin had gotten involved with anyone from this locale.

The lady apparently had a green thumb, he thought as he surveyed her small square of earth. Late summer flowers were everywhere, blooming in great untidy bursts of color all around the border of the little yard, growing through the sagging picket fence. A pink rambler rose completely blotted out the sunlight from a full half of the rickety board porch that stretched across the front of the place. There were a few rotted boards on the porch floor that had broken through and he stayed close to her front door, hoping that the owner had had the sense to keep the main entry where people walked in better repair than the rest.

He put his finger on the bell and pressed hard. No answering sound alerted the occupants of a visitor. Pulling open the torn screen door, he rapped sharply at the wooden door. A surprisingly clean white lacy curtain blocked his view through the window in the upper part of the door. Still hearing no sound of any-one walking toward the door, he rapped again. "Hello? Anyone home?"

"Just a moment." The voice was feminine, far-away and distinctly frustrated.

He waited impatiently, glancing twice at his watch before a rustling at the curtain preceded the opening of the inner door. A face stared out at him.

Garrett stared back. She wasn't what he'd expected. At all. Actually, he hadn't known what to expect, but this—this *wood nymph* wasn't it. It was a fanciful thought for a man who dealt largely in numbers, but it was strangely appropriate.

For one thing, she wasn't nearly as old as he'd expected any acquaintance of Robin's to be. For another, she was one of the most strikingly beautiful women he'd ever seen. Even with her red-gold tangle of tresses jammed into a messy pile atop her head and corkscrew curls escaping to bob wildly around her small, heart-shaped face, she was beautiful. Her eyes were an arresting vivid blue-green, large and lushly lashed, with brows that rose above them on her high forehead like perfect crescents. Her cheekbones were slanted, her little chin almost too pointy. But her mouth was full and pink in contrast to the rest of her creamy satin complexion.

And for yet a third thing, she was, well, *stacked* was the only word that sprang to mind. Beneath a soft jade T-shirt that brought out the color in her eyes and the casual jean shorts was a lithe, curvaceous figure that even the baggiest of shirts couldn't hide.

And hers wasn't baggy. If anything, it had been washed once too often and had shrunk a size or two. The shirt was ripped across one shoulder, baring an expanse of silky-looking skin that made him want to reach through the torn screen and touch. In her hands she carried a handful of multicolored ribbon that fluttered and clung to her body as she moved. One silky strand had flipped upward to curl around her left breast, outlining the full, rounded mound and his gaze followed the path of the ribbon as he tried to fathom her connection to his stepfather.

Abruptly he faced the truth he'd been hoping hadn't been true at all: this woman must have been Robin's lover. Why else would he have been seeing someone so young and...unsuitable for him?

Belatedly he realized that he was staring at her. He flushed, annoyed with himself.

"May I help you?" Her gaze was direct and unsmiling, her words clearly enunciated in a prim British accent.

"I'm looking for Ana Birch."

"You've found her." Her voice was deliberate. "I'm on a bit of a schedule—" schedule came out "shedule," in the British fashion "—and I'm really not interested in whatever it is you're selling." She began to turn away.

"Oh, I think you'll be interested in this," Garrett said in a grim tone, remembering why he had come to this dreary little neighborhood in search of her. "My name is Garrett Holden. Are you acquainted with Robin Underwood?"

"Garrett!" She held out a hand and her face altered immediately, breaking into a blinding smile that completely transformed her serious, intense expression into one of beauty and warmth. Lively intelligence and a hopeful light shone from her eyes as she opened the door and stepped onto the porch, looking past him. "Robin's spoken of you often. Is he with you?"

Garrett stared at her for a moment, ignoring her offered hand as her smile faltered. She didn't know. *She didn't know.* A fierce wave of anger and grief roared through him like a wind-fueled fire. "Robin's dead," he said shortly.

"Wha...?" She put a hand to her throat as ribbons slithered to the floor. She shook her head slowly, speaking carefully. "I'm sorry. I believe I must have misunderstood."

He stared at her coldly, not bothering to hide the contempt he felt. "You didn't misunderstand."

Her eyes widened, the pupils going black with shock. Every ounce of pink drained from her face, and he was absently surprised at just how much color she'd really had before. Now she was white as paper. She groped for the porch rail, then carefully lowered herself onto it in a seated position. The whole time, her gaze never left his. "Please tell me this is a very bad joke," she whispered.

He shook his head. He suppressed the feelings of guilt and sympathy that rose within him, reminding himself that this woman didn't need his sympathy. Unless it was to console her on the loss of the wealthy catch she'd been hoping to land.

"What happened?" Her voice was nearly soundless.

"Heart attack," he said succinctly. "He just didn't wake up. The doctor says he doubted he even felt anything." He didn't know why he'd added that last, except that he was human, after all, and the woman in front of him, whatever her motives, looked genuinely stricken by the news. Then again, maybe she was saying goodbye to the loss of the fortune she'd probably been expecting to harvest once she'd talked the old man around to marriage.

She was shaking her head as if she could deny the reality of his words. Straightening, she crossed her arms, hugging herself and appearing to shrink into a smaller presence. "When is the funeral?"

Nonplussed, it took him a moment to respond. Surely she hadn't expected to be invited to attend. "It was yesterday."

If it were possible for her to lose any more color, she did. She turned away from him and he could see her shoulders begin to shake. Then her knees slowly gave way and she sagged to the floor.

Garrett reacted instinctively. Leaping forward, he caught her as she crumpled. The essential male animal beneath the civility of centuries momentarily clouded his mind as his brain registered the close press of yielding female flesh, the rising scent of warm woman—

She squeaked and yanked herself away from him. She hadn't fainted, as he'd first assumed. And now her face wasn't white, it was a bright, unbecoming red as she flushed with embarrassment.

He only noted it with half his brain, because the other half was still processing the moment before.

Then sanity returned. God, he was disgusting. This woman had been his stepfather's...plaything. His seventy-three-year-old stepfather and this...how old was she? Twenty? Twenty-one? And here he was, enthralled by her body as well. He was truly disgusting. And so was she. No way could she have been sexually aroused by, or satisfied by Robin. Yuck. It didn't even bear thinking about.

She was backing away from him as his thoughts ran wild. "Excuse me, please. I have to...have to go inside."

"Wait—"

But he was too late. She'd fled, yanking open the rickety screen and the door behind it with incredible speed and slamming both behind her. He was left staring at the undulating lace curtain that covered the door's window. Ribbon still lay strewn across the porch.

He swore. "Miss Birch? I have to talk to you." He raised his voice. "Miss Birch?"

No answer.

Then he heard the faint sound of weeping. Deep, harsh, stuttering sobs underscored with unmistakable grief. The kind of sounds it would have been unmanly for him to have made, though he'd felt like it a time or two since Robin's manservant had come to him four days ago and reported that the master appeared to have passed away during the night.

Well, that killed any hope that she'd return. No woman with swollen eyes and a runny nose would willingly be seen in public. Dammit!

He pulled a business card and his gold pen from his pocket and scrawled a note across the back of it: *You are mentioned in the will. Call me.*

That ought to get results, he thought cynically as he strode back to his car, glad to be leaving the dingy, depressing area with its faint air of menace. In fact, he'd lay odds that he heard from her before the end of the day. If she thought there was money involved, the grief-stricken act would fly out the window in a hurry.

He unlocked his sleek bronze foreign car and drove back toward the beltway.

Thirty minutes later, he pulled into the quiet green oasis of the peaceful, shaded cemetery near Silver Spring where Robin had been buried the day before. Parking his car along the verge, he walked over the spongy earth to the fresh gravesite.

"Well, you've managed to surprise me, old man," he said aloud, thrusting his hands into the pockets of his suit pants. "How the hell you managed to keep up with something as young as that, I'll never know. No wonder you had a heart attack."

The flowers had wilted considerably just since yesterday in the humid July weather and he made himself a note to call the groundskeeper of the cemetery and ask him to remove them soon. He'd rather see bare earth than these pitiful reminders of mortality.

"I wasn't ready," he said gruffly. "I wasn't ready for you to go yet." It was the first time he'd allowed himself to think about what he'd lost. Dealing with the medical examiner, the funeral arrangements, and the never-ending calls from sympathetic well-wishers had helped him to avoid thinking about the loss of the man who had taken a rebellious teenage stepson in hand and given him self-respect and love. Now, the grief rose up and squeezed his chest until he could barely breathe, and he leaned heavily on the gravestone that had yet to have Robin's date of death inscribed beside his first wife's.

"Why?" he said. "What was so important about this woman that you put her in the will? Were you that lonely?"

It was possible, he supposed. Legions of aging men had been taken in by the solicitous attentions of glowing young beauties who professed devotion. He should know. Hadn't it happened to his very own father? Of course, there was one significant difference between the current situation and the past. Robin hadn't left a wife and a small child for the sake of a younger woman. Another was, of course, the age difference. Robin must have been nearly fifty years older than his paramour, a fact Garrett simply couldn't seem to wrap his mind around.

Sighing, he laid a hand on the marble of the stone, still cool even in the heat of the summer. "I don't begrudge you any happiness you might have found with someone who cared for you. But the thought of a woman taking deliberate advantage of your loneliness makes me damn mad." He paused, wondering why he felt so guilty. "If I neglected you, I am sorry," he said. True, he'd been busy in the past few years, but he'd always made time for Robin. Hadn't he?

Yes. He had, he confirmed as he searched his soul, and he shouldn't have regrets on that score. If anything, Robin had been the one who had been too busy recently for the several-times-weekly dinners they'd often shared. Robin had been the one who had had plans and had taken a rain check on a number of occasions. He'd been happier in the last year before his death than he'd been since Garrett's mother had died, his step more youthful, his still-handsome features smiling even more than usual. Garrett even had teased him about having a woman on several occasions, but Robin simply had smiled and lifted his eyebrows mysteriously...until last week.

Last Tuesday, just days before his death, Robin had responded in a different way to Garrett's teasing.

"I'll introduce you to her soon," he'd promised. "I believe you'll like her." The use of the feminine pronoun had confirmed Garrett's hunch. But he'd envisioned someone, well, someone older, more mature, a dignified, pleasant matron. *Not* the very young woman with the cover girl measurements and flawless complexion who looked young enough to be his daughter. Or even more likely, his granddaughter. True, Robin had been good-looking and modestly wealthy, in great physical shape for his age, or so everyone had thought. And it also was true that any number of lonely widows had let him know his attentions would be welcome. But it was a little too much to believe that a fresh-faced girl in her twenties would find him irresistibly attractive.

Unless she had her eye on Robin's fortune. *That* was a far more likely scenario. Robin's assets might have been modest in comparison to the huge financial coffers he, Garrett, had amassed, but Robin was definitely a wealthier man than most. It was more than possible that a young woman would look at that money and consider a few years with an older man worth the price.

He supposed he should be glad Robin hadn't married her. After Garrett's mother, Barbara, his second wife, passed away two years ago, Robin had said he would never marry again. But still...a man in his early seventies might have physical needs to fulfill. Considering he hoped to reach that age someday, he surely hoped so.

He stirred and stood, straightening his shoulders and a deep shudder of revulsion worked through him. *Don't go there.* He'd have to talk to Miss Ana Birch again, despite the deep disgust he felt at the mere thought of Robin with that nubile seductress. The lawyer who served as Robin's executor had been very clear in his instructions. There would be no discussion of the terms of Robin's will unless Miss Birch and Garrett both were present.

When he returned to the house he'd shared with his stepfather, he went straight to his study and reached for the telephone. "Miss Birch, this is Garrett Holden, Robin's stepson," he said when she answered the phone. "You are required to attend the reading of the will—"

"No." Her voice was final. "You can have anything he left me. Send whatever you need me to sign and I'll do it."

And before he could even begin another sentence, she hung up. She was giving up an inheritance?

He stared at the phone he still held, torn between wishing that he wouldn't have to see her again and annoyance at her attitude. He didn't get it. Impatiently he punched the redial button. When she said, "Hello?" he said, "You don't understand. You have to be there."

"I do not." She sounded belligerent now. "Please don't call again." And to his utter astonishment, she hung up on him a second time.

Once he'd gotten past the shock, he thoughtfully replaced the handset in its cradle. Fine. He'd go and see her again. He'd figured her out now. She must want money, and she was being coy and devious in an effort to disguise her greediness. Despite her protestations, he suspected that she already knew the provisions of the will, at least as they concerned her. Which meant she knew more than he did. He'd just have to promise her more than whatever sum Robin had already promised her and she'd get more agreeable.

He rested his elbows on his desk and speared his hands through his dark hair, massaging his scalp. He'd had a nagging headache for the past few days and it didn't seem to be getting any better. It was probably all the stress.

Once the will was settled and he didn't have so many urgent things to attend to, he promised himself a week at the cottage in Maine. The small cabin that looked out over Snowflake Lake in southern Maine had been a special place for Robin and his stepson. Garrett knew he'd built it about a quarter-century ago. He'd long suspected it had been Robin's only indulgence, the single respite he had allowed himself from the burden his first marriage had become as his wife's mental illness had progressed until she'd finally passed away.

Garrett's own mother had had little interest in spending her vacations in a rustic cottage where the principal entertainment consisted of fishing and watching the sunsets. She'd always refused to come to Maine. So the cabin had become a place where Garrett and Robin went at least once a year for what Robin laughingly had called, "Boys' Week." They swam in the frigid lake, fished and canoed around its perimeter looking for wildlife, settled on the deck with drinks and plenty of insect repellent each evening, and gone for the occasional jaunt to the surrounding tourist locations.

Yes, a week at the cottage was just what he needed. It would be difficult without Robin, but in some ways, he felt he'd be closer to his stepfather than he was here in Baltimore where they'd spent the bulk of their lives together.

He drove back into the city in early evening, thanking the long hours of daylight that kept him from making the journey in the dark. This time when he knocked, the inner door opened almost immediately.

"Miss Birch," he said before she could speak, infusing his tone with more warmth than he felt, "I apologize for the insensitive way I broke the news of Robin's passing. It's been a difficult time. May I come in and talk to you for a few moments?"

She hesitated. He couldn't see her clearly through the screen, but she'd obviously changed clothes. Now she wore a sleeveless denim jumper with a short-sleeved top beneath. Her hair was still pulled up, but now it was in a tidier, thick ponytail that bounced behind her head. To his great relief, she pushed open the door. Wordlessly she turned and retreated into the house, leaving him to catch the door and follow her.

The room he entered was a living room, furnished with comfortably overstuffed furniture in a faded flower pattern, threadbare but clean. The small space somehow managed to look uncluttered and on the one sizable wall there was an unusual collection of hats. Old hats. Elegant, vintage hats.

She shut the door behind him and he heard the hum of an air-conditioner cooling the small half-house.

He raised one eyebrow and turned to her, forcing himself to ignore the leap of his pulse at the porcelain beauty of her features. Indicating the headgear displayed on the wall, he said, "You like hats, I take it?"

She nodded. "I went through a stage where I collected them. Those were a few of my favorites that I decided to keep when I sold the rest." She waved a hand toward the sofa. "Please, have a seat. May I get you a drink?"

If this were any other occasion, he'd have been amused by her scrupulous manners. He shook his head. "No, thank you." He took a seat on the far end of the couch, expecting her to join him, but she went across the room and sat in a rocking chair.

"Thank you for seeing me," he said, though it grated that he had to be so civil. "Have you given any more thought to what I said about listening to the reading of the will?"

"I don't care about the will," she said tonelessly. "But I'd like to know where he's buried so I can visit the—the grave."

Right. And he was a little green man. "I care about the will," he said, watching her closely, "since it involves me, too."

"You can have everything." Her accent was even more obvious as she clipped off the syllables, and she met his eyes without even a hint of guile. She was good; he'd have to give her that. "I'll sign anything you wish."

"Believe me, I'd like nothing better," he told her curtly, abandoning his attempts to mollify her. What an act. "Unfortunately it's not that simple. We both have to be present for the reading of the will."

"Why?" she demanded.

He opened his mouth to answer her, but a hissing sound and a movement from his peripheral vision distracted him. Glancing over, he caught sight of a striped blur streaking up the stairs. "What's that?" he said, startled, though he was pretty sure the animal had been a cat.

"It's my cat. She's not very friendly yet."

"Yet?"

"I found her lying on the road. Someone hit her and drove away. She was still alive when I finally got to a veterinary clinic. So when she was well enough to come home, I brought her here. She's good company."

"She doesn't seem overly tame."

"She was wild, I think." Ana Birch's face had lost its impassive mask; her eyes brightened and she became more animated as she spoke of the animal. He felt an unwilling tug of attraction; she really was a beautiful woman. "But she's getting used to me."

"Why didn't you just let her go where you found her if she's so wild?"

"She needs seizure medication. She was struck in the head and the vet thinks the damage may be permanent. Besides, she's missing half her teeth on one side and she can't eat anything but very soft foods with any ease. She probably wouldn't survive out-doors.'' Then the soft loveliness faded and her fea-tures became set and unreadable once again. ''So why is it so imperative that I attend this will-reading cer-emony or whatever one calls it?''

He shrugged. ''That's the way Robin wanted it. He set it up with his lawyer and I've spoken with the man. He refuses to divulge anything unless we're both present.''

She was frowning at him, her light brown eyebrows drawn into a slanting scowl. ''So if I refuse to attend, you get nothing? Is that how it works?''

''Probably,'' he told her, though he was certain of no such thing.

''That old rotter,'' she muttered.

''I beg your pardon?'' he said, startled.

''He knew I wouldn't want anything. He knew I'd refuse, so this way at least I have to hear what he wanted me to hear or you'll lose your inheritance, too. And he knew I wouldn't let that happen.''

An unexpected pang of pure green-eyed jealousy squeezed his heart. There was no doubt in his mind now that whatever their relationship, she'd known—and understood—Robin quite well. Masking his thoughts behind an impassive expression, he focused on the only thing that mattered. ''So you'll come?''

She sighed. ''I suppose. When and where?''

When Ana arrived the next morning, Robin's step-son was already in the lawyer's waiting area. He stood with his back to her, looking out the far window as Ana came down the hall, and she observed him through the plate glass of the office front before she entered.

The set of his shoulders looked as rigid as the man's attitude. A lump rose in her throat as she thought of how certain Robin had been that Garrett would welcome her to the family. It was the only time in the short few years she'd known Robin that he'd been so completely wrong about something.

Robin. She tilted her face up to contain the tears that wanted to escape.

She couldn't believe her father was gone. They'd had so little time together. Oh, she'd known he was older than he looked. In fact, she'd been shocked when he'd told her his age on his last birthday. He had been seventeen years older than her mother. She knew her mother had been more than thirty when they met, which would have made him in his late forties. A large disparity, but at those ages, still quite plausible.

Perhaps they had finally found each other again, her father and her mother. And that thought, strangely, calmed her as nothing else had.

She glanced again at Robin's stepson, technically her own stepbrother, she supposed and as she did, he turned and saw her. When their eyes met, a small *zing* of awareness exploded along her nerve endings. She'd felt it the first time he'd come around, and the second. But now, as then, she'd brushed it away. So what if the man was attractive? He'd proven his beauty to be no more than skin-deep with his nasty attitude. Still, she couldn't help wishing they'd met under different circumstances.

The sense of loss she'd felt since he'd told her of her father's death intensified as she thought of the day he'd come to her house. For months, she'd imagined the day that Robin introduced her to Garrett. She'd built comfortable, civilized little images of a brotherly type, of the three of them sharing holiday dinners and warm, informal get-togethers.

She had never imagined that the first time they'd meet would be under these circumstances. She still couldn't accept that she'd missed Robin's funeral.

And Garrett couldn't be less brotherly if he tried. He'd been so curt and obnoxious yesterday that she'd wanted only to ignore him and hope he'd go away. And to top it all off, she'd nearly fainted like a ninny and when he'd tried to help she'd acted like a skittish virgin. Could this get any worse?

That was probably spitting in the eye of fate, she decided. For the sake of Robin's memory, she was going to try her very best to get along with Garrett.

Though they hadn't been related, he actually looked more like her father than she did. And her father had been a handsome man. Garrett's hair was dark, cut short and severe, and his face was long and leanly molded. He was dressed in an expensive-looking black suit and she suddenly realized that he strongly resembled the most recent actor to portray James Bond in the movies. Unfortunately the resemblance didn't carry over to personality. Garrett's stormy blue eyes regarded her with distinct animosity, and she wondered again what on earth she could have done to make him dislike her. As far as she knew,

Robin hadn't told him about her yet at the time of his death.

She wasn't going to let his attitude cow her, though. He'd insisted she attend this ridiculous will-reading—how archaic was that, anyhow? Why couldn't the lawyer simply have called her and told her whatever was so important? Garrett didn't appear even to have considered the fact that she might have to work, or have plans of her *own*.

In fact, both were true. She had the day off from her job as a teller at a local bank, although she did have to work this evening at the restaurant where she was a waitress. But she had planned to work today anyhow, in another sense.

Two days ago, she'd received a call from the agent who had approached her about doing a book on the history of hats after she'd given a lecture at a local college's textiles fair. The man had an editor at a New York publishing house who was very interested in seeing her ideas for the book.

The phone call had left her buoyant and giddy, although frustrated and apprehensive at the same time. She'd been thinking about the project ever since—and that's about as far as she'd gotten.

It drove her crazy that she had so little time for anything other than simply making ends meet. Since her mother's death three years ago shortly after Ana's twentieth birthday, there had been more bills to pay and less time for designing the line of hats and handbags she'd started. Almost none, in fact.

Her accessories currently were sold at two exclusive boutiques in the Baltimore area and both retailers had told her they could sell anything she could give them. Some days her fingers itched for a pencil and a sketchpad when she was struck by yet another idea or theme for her unique creations. Invariably she was in the car on the way to work, or counting money, or carrying plates of food to a table when it happened. She didn't know how she was going to do it, but she was determined to find more time to design and sew. If she had the smallest hope of becoming a serious artisan, even making a living from her work, she *had* to produce more. Acquire wider recognition.

Publishing a book would certainly help with that goal if she could find the time to fit it in.

She could have worked this morning. And yet, here she was, stuck in an office with a man who couldn't stand her. The feeling was rapidly becoming mutual.

He strode toward the door before she moved to open it, yanking it wide. "Come in. We've been waiting for you."

Irked by his inference, she made a show of checking her watch. "Goodness. You're early, too. Here I thought I'd be the one cooling my heels."

If she'd managed to irritate him, he didn't show it. "Follow me. They've reserved a conference room for us." Without waiting for her answer, he turned and swiftly moved off through the suite of offices, leaving her to follow or be hopelessly lost in the rabbit warren of corridors through which they passed. Feeling rebellious, Ana stuck out her tongue at his broad back as she hurried along behind him. Immediately she felt the urge to giggle. She'd been mocking Garrett Holden!

She would have known his name even if he hadn't been her father's stepson. He was extraordinarily wealthy, reputed to have parlayed a small stock market windfall into the immense assets he held today. In accordance with Americans' vulgar fascination with piles of money, he often made the pages of both gossipy newsmagazines as well as more serious financial tomes. His name had been linked to some very high-profile ladies from the entertainment world as well as the young women whose families inhabited the rarified world in which he lived, but there had never been one who lasted more than a few months, according to Robin.

"He's never confided in me," Robin had said to her once, "but he wasn't always so cynical about relationships. I suspect the change might have stemmed from a bad experience with a woman who wanted his money. It's amazing what a whiff of wealth will do to supposedly decent people."

Now that she'd met him, she couldn't imagine a woman actually *wanting* to spend time with Grumpy Garrett on a regular basis. She'd rather be boiled in oil.

Two

They settled into two stately leather chairs before Mr. Marrow's desk. The lawyer peered over the top of reading glasses at them after examining Ana's driver's license and being satisfied that she really was who she'd said she was.

"Robin's wishes were a bit...unusual," the man began.

"In what way?" Garrett clearly was used to being the one to direct things.

"Perhaps Mr. Marrow will tell us if you don't interrupt him," she said sweetly. When Garrett sent her a seething glance, she smiled at him, determined to show him his antagonism didn't unsettle her in the least.

The lawyer cleared his throat. "I'll dispense with the legalese and explain this in plain English. The disposition of Mr. Robin Underwood's assets is as follows: To Garrett Wilbur Holden, Robin gives all his worldly goods, possessions and monies with the exception of those specifically designated in this will.''

Wilbur? His middle name was *Wilbur?* She smothered a bubble of hysterical laughter that threatened to pop right out of her. At her side, Garrett's elegantly clad foot stopped the ceaseless tapping motion it had been making since he'd sat down. She supposed what he'd just heard had reassured him that she wasn't going to get any breathtaking bequest that would threaten his inheritance. Although why Garrett Holden needed to worry about inheriting money was beyond her. Though she was a pragmatic person who accepted the way fate had shaped her life, she couldn't help but think of the difference that even a small amount of money could have made to her.

Her attention returned to Marrow as he plowed on with his explanations. ''To Ana Janette Birch, Robin gives one half of the property known as Eden Cottage on Snowflake Lake in the state of Maine, in the county of—''

''What?'' Garrett sprang to his feet, his tone outraged. ''What kind of crazy bequest is that? It makes no sense. Why would Robin give her half the cottage?''

She sat up straighter in her chair, equally astonished at the gift. A *cottage?*

Mr. Marrow held up one finger for silence. ''Additionally, Ana is to receive a sum commensurate with the total of her rent and utility bills for the Baltimore home as well as a living allowance for the thirty-one-day period immediately after her residence in Snowflake Cottage is established."

"What?" Now it was her turn to interrupt the man. She lived in Baltimore!

"To Garrett, Robin bequeaths the other half of Eden Cottage. There is, however, a condition attached to the transfer of ownership to each of you. If each person named herein is unmarried, for a thirty-one-day period beginning no later than one week from the reading of this will, Ana Birch and Garrett Holden are to cohabitate at the cottage." The man's prim voice and stuffy language gave the word "cohabitate" overtones that echoed uncomfortably through the spacious office.

There was a dead silence in its wake. A *tense* silence.

"I hope this is Robin's idea of a joke," Garrett finally said, and there was a restrained fury in his tone that made Ana want to move her chair to the far side of the room. "He can't have been serious. Why in God's name would he want Ana and me to live together?" He turned to face her. "It's unenforceable. This can't be legal."

"I'm afraid he was deadly serious and it is fully legal, unless you married previous to the reading of this document," Marrow said. "You did not. Nor did Miss Birch. My job was to ensure that. If either of you should refuse to comply with the requests contained in the document, you both will lose the property and it will be sold, proceeds to benefit a charity also specified herein." The lawyer clearly was growing more nervous, his speech reverting to the no doubt comforting dry obfuscation of the legal language in which he dealt. "If you don't wish to accept the conditions, I'll start proceedings to liquidate the cottage and property and arrange to donate—"

"Don't start anything," Garrett said. "We need time to think about this." He paused. "Robin specifically said that she and I are to share the cottage for an entire month? And then each of us will own half of it?"

Marrow nodded.

"May I have a copy?" It wasn't a request, but a royal command.

"Of course." The older man rose. "I'll have one made for each of you right now. Excuse me." And he left the room.

Ana wished *she* could leave the room. When she glanced up, Garrett was staring at her with narrowed eyes. She bit her lip, not knowing what to say. She honestly couldn't blame him for being angry and she felt a surprising spurt of annoyance penetrate the sense of loss she felt for her father. Robin had put them both in an untenable position.

Garrett cleared his throat. "I'm taking this to another legal expert. It can't be as ironclad as that old fool wants us to think. I'm assuming you don't want to be saddled with half a cottage in Maine?"

She shook her head. "Of course not. But—"

"Good. I'll buy you out. Pay you a fair market value for your half."

"You're familiar with this place?"

It was amazing. The moment her words registered,

his face changed. There wasn't a great difference but something…softened. His eyes warmed to a glowing blue. She was astonished. The small shift in his expression made him dangerously compelling and even more seductively attractive than he already was—and he hadn't even smiled. If she were a smart woman, she'd keep him angry, because if he ever directed a look like that at her, she'd probably be his slave for life.

"Robin and I went there together every summer," he said, his eyes unfocused, his face gentler than she'd have thought a man as hard as he appeared to be could manage. "We'd fish and canoe around the lake looking for loons and eagles' nests." Then his gaze cooled as he focused on the present—on her—again. "It means a hell of a lot more to me than it ever will to you."

She wasn't so sure about that. Robin had left her half of the cottage; it must have been very special to him. What was there that he'd wanted her to see badly enough to insist that she share it with her stepbrother for a whole month? And then it struck her. The odd phrasing: "…if each person…is unmarried…"

"I think," she said hesitantly, "I think he might have been trying to set us up."

"Set us up?" Garrett repeated. "As in romantically? You and me?" There was a wealth of disbelief and disgust in his tone. "That's an extraordinarily self-serving bit of wishful thinking. Robin never would have done anything so…so…distasteful."

She flinched, sliced to the bone by his cruelty, not understanding it. "What have I ever done—"

"Or maybe," he said, "it's hopefulness. Did you really think you could hook me after Robin died?"

She sucked in a quick gasp of shock, both at the crude question and the hateful tone in which it was delivered. "I didn't think enough about you to consider the idea." Her voice was shaking and she hated the tears that sprang to her eyes. "And even if I had, you can rest assured that meeting you would have changed my mind instantly."

"Good." He was infuriatingly unfazed by her verbal arrows. "I'll buy out your half of the cottage and as soon as we sign the papers, neither one of us will ever have to see the other again."

"Fine." She stood and marched to the door, not waiting for the lawyer's return. "I can't think of anything I'd like more than signing you out of my life."

It wasn't until she got home that she calmed down enough to think about the ugly scene again. And when she did, her hand flew to her mouth in stunned shock at the implications of his behavior. He didn't know who she was. Or, to put it more accurately, he didn't know *what* she was.

Did you really think you could hook me after Robin died? Emphasis on the *me*.

He thought she was Robin's…his…his lover!

Word by word, expression by expression, she reviewed each moment of the three times they'd met. And as she did, her anger grew. And grew, and *grew*.

How dare he jump to a conclusion like that? Oh, she could admit that it might not be such an illogical one to make, but she knew he'd known Robin for years, ever since Robin had married his mother. How could he not have trusted Robin's integrity? How could he even imagine Robin would take up with a girl of her age? She was *furious* with Garrett for Robin's sake as much as for her own.

Nasty, bloody-minded pervert. There wasn't a word bad enough to describe him, with his sewage-for-brains stupid assumptions. If only she had some way to make him sorry. How she wished she were a man. How she wished she could—

She could! She had in her hands a wonderfully wicked way to pay him back for his rude, callous actions.

She actually rubbed her hands together, cackling with glee as she decided how best to flummox Mr. Gutter-mind Garret Holden. Obviously that property meant quite a bit to him. He'd shared special moments there with her father. She suffered a pang of conscience for a moment. Her father had loved Garrett. God knew why, but he had. Still…Garrett apparently hadn't loved or understood Robin as he should have or he never would have believed for a minute that his stepfather would have an affair with her.

And that reminder solidified her desire to pay him back. She nearly leaped for the phone and called him, but thank the Lord she came to her senses before she did. She could wait. She would wait, until *he* was forced to come to *her*.

He called her the next day, full of unctuous courtesy. It was amusing. She wondered what he *really* wanted to say, but when he asked if he could come by that evening, she merely agreed. "It'll have to be after ten, though," she said. "I'm working tonight and I won't be home until then."

"I didn't realize you had a job." His tone was stiff.

Oh, this was too good a chance to miss. "Of course. My schedule changes from week to week, so I never know whether I'm going to be working days or nights or both."

There had been an ominous silence on the other end of the line and she'd had to bite her lip to keep from laughing at his expense. Oh, she couldn't *wait* to tell him who she was. He was going to feel so foolish and she would make certain she was there to see the moment.

But aloud, all she said was, "So I'll see you around ten, then?"

"Ten it is." And he hung up without even a fare-well.

That evening, luck was with her and she didn't have any late tables, so she was home shortly before ten. She took a quick shower to rid herself of the food odors, dried her hair enough to scrunch wild curls around her face, and sprayed herself liberally with her favorite scent, an expensive one she wore rarely but figured was appropriate for this evening. Then she dressed in a white silk blouse cut in a discreet vee, a slim, short black skirt, and a pair of high-heeled pumps that made her legs look a mile long. Battle gear. She supposed she might look like an expensive hooker, if that's what one was predisposed to think. The doorbell rang just as she was walking down her narrow staircase.

"Good evening," she said as she opened the door. "Please come in."

"Your home needs some work," Garrett said without even greeting her.

"Yes. It's getting rather shabby," she agreed.

"The porch needs to be repaired," he pointed out, "and the whole place could stand to be painted."

"I'm sure it could." She smiled brightly at him. "Would you like to sit down?"

He came in and took the exact same seat he'd taken before on her couch. "You could do a lot to this place with the money I'll pay you for the cabin."

"I'm sure I could," she agreed. "If I owned it."

She'd managed to surprise him and it showed. "You don't? I just assumed..."

"You're quite good at that," she said pleasantly.

She watched with gleeful eyes as he fought back a snarl. Finally he said, "If you don't own it, who does?"

"The landlord." She waited a moment until he looked ready to explode. Then she smiled innocently. "We moved here from England when I was ten and my mother bought the place. It was a reasonably nice little neighborhood then." Her smile faded. "Mother died three years ago and I needed money. I didn't care to stay here permanently. The area's getting seedier and seedier. So I sold it with a provision that I be able to rent it for up to five years." But she didn't tell him about her mother and Robin. She might never. He didn't deserve to know.

"All right," he said impatiently. "So you don't have to take care of a property. That should make the money even more appealing. You can bank it. Travel.''

''Go back to school,'' she suggested.

His eyebrows rose. ''If that interests you.'' He paused. ''Does it?''

''No,'' she said serenely. ''I don't need additional education to further my life plan.''

''I just bet you don't,'' he murmured.

Now that she knew what he was thinking, cryptic comments like that made sense. He'd been insulting her steadily and until recently, she hadn't even known it. She felt her blood begin to boil again and she pushed the anger away, concentrating instead on this chance to rattle him. ''So when do we leave?'' she asked.

''What?''

''When do we leave?'' she repeated as if he were a bit slow. ''For Eden Cottage. What a pretty name. I can't wait to see it. It must have been a very special place for Robin to consider it Eden.''

''*We* aren't going anywhere,'' he said. ''I've already dropped off the will at another legal firm. I expect them to be able to get us out of that insane clause. Then I'll buy you out and we'll be done with it.''

''Buy me out?'' She widened her eyes. ''Oh, did I forget to mention my change of plans?''

He regarded her with distrust. ''Apparently. What change?''

She cleared her throat, enjoying the moment. ''I've decided not to sell my half. It was special to Robin so I've decided to keep it.''

"I thought you needed money." His voice was tight, as if someone were squeezing his neck hard enough to affect his vocal cords.

"I do, but not that desperately," she said. "If we go to Maine for a month, it's essentially an all-expenses-paid vacation for me. We can chat at the end of that time if I've changed my mind." She stood. "I hate to throw you out, but I've had an exhausting day."

He stood, too, but instead of heading for the door he stalked across the room in her direction. "If I can get that clause changed, you'll have half a cabin and *no* free ride. And I'll expect you to pay half of all taxes and expenses related to the cabin's upkeep."

"Even if you get that clause changed," she said blithely, "I probably still will go. Maybe I'll even move there permanently. Owning half a cabin in Maine has to be less expensive than renting in Baltimore."

He practically was foaming at the mouth, he was that angry. She watched his hands clench and unclench at his sides, fascinated by his battle for control. "We're not done discussing this," he warned her before he stomped out.

He heard from the other lawyer late the next afternoon and when he ended the conversation, it was all he could do not to throw the phone across the room. His temper was short these days and he knew at least part of the reason why. He hadn't slept well since Robin had died. Though he'd managed not to wallow in grief during the day, he'd had vivid dreams of his stepfather every night, dreams that always ended with Robin closing a door in his face or disappearing around a corner.

It didn't take a psychologist to figure out that he was trying to work through his sense of loss at Robin's unexpected death. Still, between the lack of rest and this business with that stupid will Robin had made... Once again he went back over the will's specific provisions. Every lawyer who had seen the language of the will had been of the same opinion: unless there was some clear question about Robin's sanity at the time he had it drawn up, it was perfectly legal, perfectly enforceable.

Since Robin unquestionably had been quite sane, it looked as if there was no way to win a challenge to his wishes.

He sighed, the anger draining from him. How in hell was he going to stand thirty-one days in Maine with her? He couldn't imagine being cooped up in the small cottage with Ana Birch for more than four weeks. Still, he supposed there was no use in prolonging the inevitable. He'd survive it.

When he called, Ana answered her phone. "Hello?"

"I've had an answer from the other lawyer about Robin's will." He didn't bother to identify himself or to wait for her to speak. He hated eating crow but he supposed he'd had it coming. "It can't be changed. So we're going to be stuck with each other."

"When do we leave?" She didn't sound smug or superior, just interested.

"*I'm* leaving tomorrow morning. I can't speak for

you.'' Surely she didn't think he'd spend sixteen hours in a car with her. ''But the sooner you get up there, the faster this farce will be over.''

He hung up and immediately called his house-keeper to instruct her to start packing. Now that he'd made up his mind, he wanted to get to the cottage as fast as possible. Before Ana, that was for sure. He had a sneaking suspicion that if she arrived first, she might just take his favorite bedroom out of spite.

The following evening, he pulled off the small country road and took the long central lane back to the smaller, rougher track that wound another half-mile along the lakeshore to Eden Cottage. There was a porch light on, waiting to greet him through the dusk, and he reminded himself to give the caretakers a bonus next month. The old man and his wife who looked after the place had cleaned it and brought in a few groceries earlier as he'd asked when he'd called to tell them he was coming.

He'd left at dawn and driven with only the most necessary stops the whole day. He was glad it was summertime, still light outside. He got out of the car and stretched, looking down the steep hillside at the flashes of silvery water revealed through the white-trunked birches. He'd pushed himself for a reason. Much later and he'd have had to wait until morning to see this view.

The cottage was perched above the lake with decks on three sides. It was surrounded by towering trees and from the back, looked quite unprepossessing. It had been built into the hill so that the second-floor section that jutted out to the back had a wide garage-style door at what was ground level there, so that the boats and outside furniture and supplies could be stored there through the winter.

He walked down the hill a little way and stepped out onto a rocky outcrop above a small pebble-beached cove. *Ahhh.* He took a deep, cleansing breath of the fresh, pine-scented air. "It's good to be here," he said aloud. As he stood motionless, absorbing the utter peace that was one of the hallmarks of the little lake, the eerie laugh of a loon floated out over the water.

Garrett chuckled in response. This wouldn't be so bad. Even though he'd arranged to have an office's worth of equipment, including fax and computer, delivered tomorrow, he'd still feel like he was on an extended vacation. But the momentary buoyancy faded as he envisioned himself sharing the small rooms with Robin's little fling.

The stutter of a poorly tuned engine could be heard in the distance, and he looked around, distracted from his annoyance. The sound was rare enough to make him scan the lake with a frown. Usually, back this far, there was little to suggest other humans were around. Only canoes and rowboats were allowed on the lake and there was a bare handful of other homes scattered along the shores. When summer ended, nearly all of those would empty out as summer residents returned to their real lives again.

The engine grew louder instead of fading, and he turned. It almost sounded as if someone were heading toward his cottage. But unless the caretaker had forgotten something, he couldn't imagine why anyone would be back here. There were clear No Trespassing signs posted both at the end of his small lane and at the larger one that led to the road.

He surged up the bank, reaching his own sturdy four-wheel-drive vehicle just as headlights played across the cottage and red brake lights flared. A door opened and a figure straightened from the driver's seat of a small, battered-looking car.

"This is absolutely beautiful!" Ana Birch said.

Garrett just stared at her. How in the hell had she managed to get organized fast enough to arrive here at practically the same time he had? He'd never known a woman who could pack and travel in less than a day's time. His mother would have needed at least a week to get ready. And that would have been pushing it.

"Have you been here long?" She bent and touched her toes in one lithe motion, drawing his eyes to the long, smooth line of her back beneath the T-shirt she wore. As she placed her palms flat on the ground and swayed from side to side to stretch out her back, her bottom stuck up in the air in an incredibly provocative manner. He caught himself in the middle of wondering just how limber she really was and banished the thought. She might have bewitched Robin but he, Garrett, knew what she was.

"I—ah, just arrived." His voice sounded rough and uneven to his own ears. "How did you get here so fast?"

She shrugged, straightening and flipping her hair back over her shoulders, drawing his gaze to the shining, curly mass. "I didn't really have much to worry about," she told him. "I packed everything I thought we'd need, stuffed the cat in a box—"

"The cat! I never said anything about sharing my cabin with a cat."

She shrugged. "I'll just have to keep her in my half, then. As I was saying, I hopped in my car late last night and started driving. When I stopped for breakfast, I called the bank and the restaurant and quit, effective immediately. I can get another job or two like that easily enough when I get back if I need it."

"Jobs? You worked for a bank *and* a restaurant?"

"Some of us don't have a fortune at our disposal," she told him tartly. "What on earth did you think I did for money?"

The question fell into the space between them like a hand grenade with the pin ready to fall out. He bit his tongue, knowing that if he said what he'd thought, there would be open warfare in the cabin for the next month. It was going to be bad enough as it was without picking a fight with her.

"Never mind." She turned away and walked around to the trunk of her car. "I already know the answer to that."

There was an odd, wistful tone in her voice that made him, for one strange moment, feel guilty for the way he'd treated her. Then he reminded himself that she was nothing more than a gold digger, snagging an old man and talking him into putting her in his will. Two jobs...no wonder she was looking for an easier way to make a living. She hadn't really loved

Robin, he was sure. He'd had his own experience with the fickle nature of a woman's love for anything but money, and nothing could convince him otherwise.

"Why do you have two jobs?" He opened his car door as he spoke and lifted out the suitcases.

"Employers don't want to pay benefits so they get around it by hiring part-time help," she said succinctly. She shrugged, and lifted out a large box. "The flexibility works just as well for me."

He started down the path. "Follow me and I'll give you the nickel tour of the cottage. I had the caretakers clean and open it earlier today." But he couldn't keep himself from wondering why she worked two low-paying jobs. She seemed bright enough. Surely she could find something more suitable. *She did,* answered his cynical side. *Bewitching an old man.*

Unaware of his thoughts, she said, "Good idea." She hefted her box with both hands. "I'll have to go and meet them. Did you tell them I'd be arriving?"

"No," he said shortly.

There was silence behind him as they came to the porch. He set down the bags and unlocked the door, then picked them up and shouldered his way through the door, leaving her to follow with her unwieldy box. She wasn't there by his choice, he told himself fiercely, and he wasn't going to spend thirty-one days being courteous, holding doors and carrying everything in sight. In fact, it was probably better if they established ground rules first thing.

He headed straight for the stairs, ignoring her, and took his bags to his bedroom. When he came down again, she was still standing in the living room, looking out through the plate glass at the lake. It was nearly dark now so he knew she couldn't see much.

He said, "The bedroom to the left at the top of the stairs is mine. You can have the other one that has a lake view. The one to the back is—" he caught himself "—was Robin's den."

She nodded.

"This is the living room and back there is the dining area. Those doors lead to the deck. The kitchen's through here and—" he moved through the house "—this is my office. There's a half bathroom in the hall and a full one upstairs. Laundry room is opposite the downstairs bath." He paused as he realized just how intimate this enforced cohabitation was going to be. "Tomorrow we'll make up a schedule of who gets the bathroom and the kitchen at what times. You'll have to help chop and stack wood, too."

Her eyebrows rose. "You don't buy it by the cord?"

He shook his head. "Nope. A lot of it's broken limbs we salvage from the previous winter's storms. If you want to share this place fifty-fifty, you'll have to share half the work." He doubted she was used to lifting a finger to do much more than some light cleaning. After all, she'd sold her own home rather than deal with maintenance and upkeep. Cleaning. "The caretaker's wife comes in once a week to clean," he told her, "but you'll have to do your own laundry, dishes and pick up any messes you make."

She simply nodded.

There was an awkward silence.

"Well," he said. "I guess I'll finish unloading."

Ana awoke to the sound of a bird trilling insistently right outside her window the next morning. The quality of the light coming through her window told her it still was very early. She'd been exhausted after the long drive and unloading her car last night, and she hadn't expected to wake at dawn, but she knew she wouldn't be able to go back to sleep now.

She threw back the light blanket and sheet with which she'd made her bed last night. Roadkill, the cat, leaped off the foot of the mattress where she'd been sleeping with a startled hiss and disappeared beneath the bed. She chuckled. "Relax, girl. I bet you'll come out of there fast enough when I return bearing food." She sat up and put her feet on the floor. *Brrr!* Even in midsummer, the night was cool.

Sliding her feet into sandals, she went to the window. Her bedroom looked out over the lake, and from this floor, she could see the earliest of the sun's rays making the water sparkle and dance, casting outsize shadows from anything in its path. The cabin was situated on the west side of the little lake, facing the sun, and its warmth was just beginning to steal over the horizon. She'd stopped at the little general store for directions and soda last night, and the clerk had told her the lake was small. But looking north and south, she couldn't see either end. Across the lake, there was a wooded shore. Farther down, just one other house peeked from between the trees, its dock floating out from the shore into the water.

A dock. She looked down and saw that Eden Cottage had a dock as well. The sight automatically brought a lump to her throat as childhood memories came flooding back. When she was young, her mother had rented a cabin along the Choptank River each summer for an entire week. It was their one annual splurge. Her mother, Janette, had loved the water and had taught Ana to swim as a very small child. They'd rowed on the river, swam and dived, held weenie roasts on their small stretch of pebbled beach and laid on the dock stargazing after dark.

Those times had been among the best of her life. They'd been anonymous vacationers, not a weird artist from England and her illegitimate child.

She dashed the tears away, annoyed with herself. Those had been good times. There was no reason to cry over them.

But oh, how she missed her mother sometimes.

That thought brought back another memory, and she almost laughed aloud in the quiet morning silence of her new house. Her new *half* a house, she corrected herself. Which half of the dock was hers? The boat? The lake? As she grabbed a towel and went down the stairs on tiptoe so as not to wake her grumpy stepbrother—who probably would be even grouchier if she woke him at dawn—she had the whimsical thought that they ought to buy a huge roll of fluorescent orange tape so that they could mark off their boundaries. Because she was fairly sure she was going to have trouble remembering where she was and wasn't allowed to tread.

Except on Garrett's toes. There would be no avoiding that.

She stole out of the house, cussing the squeaking screen door. *Oil for you later, buddy,* she promised. The path from the cottage down to the lakeshore was steep and stony, covered with a slippery layer of pine needles.

Once on the tiny crescent of water-worn rocks that served as a beach, she stood for a moment, inhaling deeply and enjoying the first warmth of the sun on her face. It was going to be a beautiful day. Despite Garrett's unfriendliness, she knew she could be happy here.

She crossed the rocks and walked out onto the dock. Looking up and down the lake, she could see no one. Perfect! She slid her feet out of her sandals, then quickly removed the oversize T-shirt in which she'd slept. Beneath it, she wore nothing. The air was warm and fresh on her body and the sensation brought back more memories from her childhood. Since she didn't know how deep the water was, she used the ladder at the end of the dock to lower herself into the lake, shivering with cold at first.

It was invigorating, though, and she began to swim strongly, energetic strokes up and down past the dock, until she had warmed up again. Garrett hadn't said anything about the lake, whether there were strong currents or hidden rocks, so she stayed fairly close to the dock, although she was an excellent swimmer and probably could have swum to the far shore and back again. At least, she could after a little training. It had been a long time since she'd done any regular swimming.

Finally she was ready to get out of the water. The sky was growing lighter and she was afraid someone might come by if she lingered any longer. As she put her hands on the ladder rungs, she cast an intent, nervous glance up at the house, but nothing stirred. She was pretty sure Garrett was still sleeping. Quickly she climbed the ladder and reached for her towel, drying herself as best she could, then pulling her T-shirt over her head and pushing her arms into the sleeves before wrapping the towel around her. Her body was still wet and the fabric clung to her. To-morrow, she'd have to wear a robe.

Oh, it was so wonderful here! The moment she'd walked into the cottage, she'd known she couldn't simply sell her half. She'd said that the other day solely to get under Garrett's hide, because it served him right for being so judgmental and hateful. But now...she didn't think she'd ever want to sell it. Not even to Robin's beloved stepson. Robin had left half of this beautiful retreat to her, his daughter, for a reason.

Her good mood was dampened as she thought of her father. She'd gone to the cemetery three times before this abrupt change of address, and though the fresh grave was mute testimony to the reality of her loss, she still couldn't believe he was gone. She was certain that if he'd lived longer, he'd have brought her up here. Thinking of him, trying to imagine him in this place made her eyes burn with the tears she didn't want to start shedding again. She'd barely met him and already she'd lost him. For a heart that had craved the love of a father throughout her whole life, it was a terrible blow. As she hurried up the path to the house, the lump that so quickly rose to her throat these days made it hard to swallow.

Three

Garrett stood at the large plate glass window in the living room, his body quickening with elemental male interest. He still wasn't sure what had awakened him, but he was damn glad he hadn't succumbed to the urge to go back to sleep. He set his coffee cup down on the windowsill, shaking his head in disbelief and pure sensual appreciation.

There were some experiences every man ought to have before he died and a moment like this was one of them. It was no wonder Robin had been taken in by this temptress, he thought as he watched Ana prepare to emerge from the water. If he didn't know what women like her really were after, he might have been hoodwinked himself in similar circumstances.

The water receded as she steadily climbed the ladder down at the dock. She had an absolutely beautiful body, with high, plump breasts and a tiny, nipped-in waist that flared to smoothly rounded hips and long, slender thighs and legs. Everything, however, was scaled down to perfect proportion for a woman as petite as she was. She probably wasn't more than five foot two, if that. He really ought to look away. He felt uncomfortably like a voyeur…but there was no power in the world that could have torn his gaze away from her just then.

Besides, he reasoned, she'd gone swimming in the nude, right out in plain view in the lake. There could be a dozen people watching her right now, for all she knew. If she hadn't been splashing so much as she swam back and forth, he might never have noticed her in the first place. And if she'd worn a bathing suit like any normal woman, he'd never have stayed glued to the window like this.

He completely disregarded the fact that he'd swum nude in the very same place more times than he could count. He was a man.

He hastily moved away from the window as she came up the path in the clinging, wet T-shirt and large towel. She already thought he was pond scum; what would she think if she realized he'd been watching her?

Why should you care?

He didn't. Of course not. But he headed for the kitchen and began getting himself a bowl of cereal. She was nothing but an interloper, a minor inconvenience, a blip on the radar screen of his life. He knew what she'd said about not selling the place but he also knew she'd get tired of being hidden away up here in the woods real quick once the novelty wore off. And then, when he made her a handsome offer for her half as soon as the time was up, she'd take the money and get out of his life for good.

Sort of the way Kammy had vanished, except that he wasn't stupid enough to be in love with this woman and he wouldn't be devastated when she left. He snorted in disgust. He hadn't thought of Kammy in…well, one hell of a long time. She'd been nothing but another blip on the radar screen, he assured himself. Only difference was, he'd learned a lesson from her: some women would do anything for money.

The squeak of the door warned him that Ana was coming into the house, and he made a point of pouring milk onto his cereal and replacing the container in the refrigerator as she came into the kitchen.

"Good morning." Her voice sounded distinctly wary. "Have you been awake long?"

"Long enough." He deliberately didn't look at her. He already knew she was wearing the wet T-shirt with a large towel wrapped around her sarong-style over top of it, and that her wet hair was clipped atop her head. And he wasn't going to ask her any additional questions that would necessitate further conversation, like how the water was. The less contact he had with her, the better.

There was a short silence, as if she were trying to decipher his meaning. Then she said, "That cereal looks good." She turned to the cupboard and began looking through the dishes. "Where are the bowls?"

"Third cabinet on the left from the sink." He kept his voice cool and casual. "Did you pick up any groceries last night? I left the right side of the refrigerator for your food. Same with the shelves in the pantry. We won't be able to split up the dishes easily— there's only one of most of the cooking utensils—but if we each clean up as soon as we're done using them, we should be able to keep out of each other's way.''

She set down a bowl and turned slowly to face him, her face a porcelain study in disbelief and something that looked suspiciously like…hurt? ''Are you telling me not to eat your food?''

''Of course not,'' he said smoothly. ''If you haven't laid in supplies yet, feel free to use some of mine. The store opens at ten, I believe.''

''I assumed,'' she said in her precise little accent, ''that we would share meals and food expenses. Wouldn't that be easier than cooking for one all the time?''

''Not for me,'' he said promptly. ''I don't want to have to worry about stopping work to make dinner or coming to the table at a certain time. My hours aren't particularly regular.''

She was still staring at him and there was a clear look of doubt mixed in with the shock. She knew he was lying, knew he simply didn't want to have anything to do with her. As he watched, her gaze dropped and she bit down on her lower lip. Turning back to the cupboard, she slowly replaced the bowl she'd removed and started out of the room.

''Hey,'' he said. ''I told you to feel free to use my stuff until the store opens.''

''Don't be silly.'' She didn't even stop. ''I wouldn't dream of imposing like that.''

He was not going to let the pathetic droop of those shoulders or the quaver in her rich, round tones arouse his sympathy, he lectured himself. She was a hell of an actress. She must have been, to fool Robin so completely. Still, he couldn't quiet the guilty feeling that made him sorry he'd chased her away. She hadn't even eaten any breakfast—no! That was no concern of his. "I'll make up a tentative schedule today," he called after her, "for us to share the common rooms and the light cleaning. You can look over it and we can make changes if something doesn't work for you."

She was through the living room and halfway up the stairs now and he heard her mutter something beneath her breath, though he couldn't make out the words. Somehow he doubted it was a compliment on his efficiency.

He barely saw her for the rest of the day. He took the canoe out of storage and maneuvered it down to the beach. It was a good thing he was the size he was. Someone as petite and delicate as his new housemate could never have done this alone. He felt rather magnanimous. Even though she hadn't helped him, he wasn't going to begrudge her the use of the small craft.

He caught a glimpse of Ana while he was supervising the deliverymen who were bringing his computer equipment through the main entry into the hall and right around the corner into his office. She was staggering down the hill from her car with two huge suitcases. To his surprise, she didn't come through the open door, but disappeared through the other entry that led directly into the kitchen. He saw her repeating the action and several times, heard her footsteps moving up and down the stairs. Shortly after that, she came out and got into her compact car and chugged off out the lane. To the store, he presumed.

After the delivery guys left, he got everything set up the way he liked it, and then sat down to deal with e-mail. His assistant had gotten him set up with the local service provider and so he was able to connect immediately. By then, it was well past lunchtime, so he went downstairs and made himself a couple of sandwiches and some instant lemonade, then carried them back up to his office. The refrigerator was still bare except for the few things he'd bought. He'd have to drive into town later for a full load of groceries. While he ate, he roughed out a tentative schedule for using the kitchen, the laundry and the bathroom. He figured Ana could schedule herself around him, or if she had some real problem with one of the times he'd appropriated, they could discuss it. He was a reasonable guy.

Ana still hadn't come back by the time he left to drive into town. He was only aware of it because she shared his home. Maybe she'd gotten lost. She'd never been up here before. A lot of the little winding roads looked alike. If she'd lost her way or had an accident, he would be the logical one for her to call.

Then he remembered the way her lower lip had quivered before she'd bitten fiercely on it in the kitchen earlier. No, she wouldn't call him. Once again the guilt rose and this time he couldn't ignore the little voice that asked: *How would Robin feel about the way you've been treating Ana? He raised you to be a gentleman.*

All right. He could admit that he'd been a real bastard. He'd try harder to be more tolerant, if not outright kind, to her. After all, Robin had cared for her. And as he thought of the spring in the old man's step and his good spirits in the last year of his life, he had to admit that she'd made Robin happier than he'd been since Garrett's mother had died over two years ago.

Whoever, *whatever,* she was, Ana must have been good to Robin. He supposed that was something to be grateful for.

Ana was delighted all out of proportion over the simple discovery of an exceptionally well-stocked fabric and craft store in town. She hadn't needed much, but how wonderful to know it was close enough that if she ran out of something, she wouldn't have to drive halfway through New England to find a store that stocked it. And she'd made her first new friends in Maine.

The proprietor of the store was delighted to meet her and quickly introduced himself. Teddy Wilkens was a young man who didn't look much older than she was. When he found out she was going to be living in the area for a while, he quickly pressed a little buzzer that she could hear faintly, echoing in some other part of the two-story shop.

"We live upstairs. We just bought this place at the beginning of the season from a couple who wanted to retire to Florida. It's a thriving business and we're excited about the possibilities," Teddy told her as he carefully wrapped and tied her purchases into a large bundle. "Unfortunately my wife is having a difficult pregnancy and doesn't see many people. She'll love it if you can stay and visit for a few minutes."

"That would be lovely." And she meant it. Just then, a hugely pregnant young woman came into the shop through a door in the back. "Nola, this is Ana Birch, who's living out on Snowflake Lake."

"Pleased to meet you." Nola Wilkens smiled warmly.

"You, also," Ana said, "but please, don't stand on my account." She pointed to a pair of rocking chairs set in a corner of the store. "Why don't we go over there and visit?"

Nola waddled ahead of her and carefully lowered herself into a chair. Ana learned that they were from Virginia originally, and that this was Nola's first child but that they'd just learned she was expecting twins, though they had chosen not to learn the sex of the babies. She was due in the early part of September.

"And that's if I go to term," Nola said. "The doctor thinks I'll probably deliver early. So I could have three weeks of this left, or seven, depending on what happens."

"Please let me know when they arrive," Ana told her. "If I'm still here, I'll bring you some meals in exchange for a chance to cuddle a baby."

Nola laughed. "I have a feeling we'll be so glad for an extra pair of hands that *we'll* want to feed *you*."

The young woman was cheerful but obviously tired and uncomfortable. As she took her leave, Ana decided she wouldn't wait for the babies to arrive. She'd take Teddy and Nola a meal the next time she came into town.

The cottage was dark and Garrett's truck was gone when she pulled to a halt at the top of the hillside above the cottage. *Good.* She already was sick to death of his hostility. Before she'd come into the kitchen earlier, she'd been so stupidly optimistic that they could live together amicably for the next four weeks. He'd wasted no time in bursting that little fantasy bubble. She'd bet he didn't even know the word amicable existed. Fuming, as angry as she'd been when she left, she slammed canned goods down on the counter as she unloaded grocery bags. Then she saw the schedule he'd left on the kitchen table. It was a neat grid of the days of the week with each hour in a separate space. He'd written in the times he wanted the kitchen and bathroom. Across the bottom was a note in a strong, masculine hand: *If any of these are a problem, we'll negotiate.*

Negotiate? Negotiate, her fanny. He wanted war, he'd get war. She hunted a pencil out of a drawer and began to scribble on the schedule, muttering to herself.

She was a reasonable person. Generally kind, inoffensive, thoughtful. Teddy and Nola Wilkens certainly hadn't found anything objectionable about her. But Garrett had gone out of his way to be as hateful as anything she could have imagined. Why? Why was he so sure she'd been Robin's lover? *That* made her madder than anything. It was insulting to her, but even worse, it was insulting to Robin. Garrett had known the man for years; how could he imagine Robin would engage in an affair with a woman decades younger than himself, much less include her in his will?

She finished bringing in her groceries and put everything away in her designated spaces. Just like a parking lot at an office. Park here, stay out of that space. Yes, she surely was going to make the man sorry he'd started this, she thought as she went to her room for the recipe box she'd brought. Crab dip would be the first salvo. Tomorrow, she'd make that fabulous chicken-broccoli casserole that filled an entire house with aroma. She could make an extra one for Teddy and Nola. It was a good thing she'd gotten that big package of chicken on sale. And she'd make pies with the Michigan cherries she'd found at that produce stand. Ha! Take that.

She really, really hoped that Garrett's cooking skills were limited to grilling and fixing things out of a box.

Then the guilt struck and her angry thoughts drained away. She was mourning Robin. How must Garrett feel? He'd lived with him, had loved him since he was a young teenager. He was grieving, too, and it wasn't unbelievable to think that his boorish behavior was born of his grief. Everyone dealt with losing a loved one differently. Garrett had been the one to find him, the one to deal with all the funeral arrangements, the one left holding all the responsibilities. He'd moved through denial, the stage she figured she still was clinging to, and perhaps now he was angry.

And who better to take it out on than her? She might not like the conclusion he'd jumped to about her character, but she could forgive it. And she would. Tomorrow she would tell him that she was Robin's daughter and set this whole mess straight.

Feeling a lot better, she went back out to her car and brought in the things she'd bought from Teddy. She took them upstairs and into the room that had been Robin's den, where she'd stored her other supplies earlier in the day. It was an ideal workspace, with enormous windows on three sides to offer plenty of light as well as to give adequate ventilation when she was working with toxic-smelling substances like glue. In addition, there was an extraordinarily good overhead lighting system. She knew Robin hadn't had an artistic bone in his body or she'd have thought this space was designed to be a craft or hobby room of some kind.

The room contained a large television, a top-notch stereo and a few pieces of comfortable furniture, but there also was a lot of unused open space. At the far end, beneath the wide window, a large table stood—perfect for her to cut fabric and lay out design ideas. And there was room enough beside it for the sewing machine in its portable cabinet that she'd brought along. A sizable wet bar was built into a countertop beneath which there was a plethora of cabinets that stretched across the whole wall beneath the window. It was perfect for her supplies and for cleaning up.

And an oversize closet with louvered doors along one wall was completely empty.

She set up her workspace, unpacking her sewing machine and arranging her fabrics and decorative accessories. A surge of pleasure ran through her as she fondled a piece of satiny burgundy felt and she had a sudden image of a subtly elegant clutch purse. Pair it with a petite pillbox with that black feather wrapped around the brim... It was a welcome relief from the blank lack of creative energy she'd been experiencing since Garrett had hurled the news of Robin's death at her four days ago.

Four days! It felt as if it had been much longer than that. She felt the tears welling again. For most of her life, she'd thought her father was dead. Her mother had spoken of him rarely, and Ana hadn't had the courage to ask of him often. On the few occasions when she had, Janette's eyes invariably would fill with such a desolate sadness that Ana knew, without a doubt, that her mother still loved the man who had fathered her. Ana herself had known only that he had been an American, that they had met a little more than a year before her birth, that they had never married but that they had loved each other deeply. The beautifully tragic landscapes for which her mother had become famous were a reflection of her feelings.

Early in her career, Janette had been a portrait artist. Ana had four pieces of her mother's portraiture: one done in soft, lovely oils of herself as a child asleep in a pram, the other two quick sketches of subjects for whom she'd later painted formal family portraits. The fourth piece was the one she cherished most: a charcoal self-portrait her mother had done of herself with Ana peeking around the edges of Janette's long, flowing skirt as she sat at an easel. Ana had been less than two when the sketch had been done. They had moved back to England, where Ana's grandparents had lived, shortly afterward. Ana had other pictures, photographs, of her mother, but this one, done by Janette's own hand, was the dearest possession she owned.

She had nothing so personal by which to remember Robin.

She shook her head as the tears fell, blinded by her scalding grief.

And jumped a mile in the air when the door banged open a moment later.

Garrett loomed in the door of her new workroom, narrowing his eyes against the bright lights. "Where were you all day?" he demanded. Then he paused, clearly unsettled when he saw her struggling for composure.

"Out," she said shortly, annoyed that he'd caught her in tears. She turned her back on him.

His footsteps advanced into the room. "What is all this?" His voice didn't sound pleased.

"My work," she said, still keeping her back to him as she used the hem of her T-shirt to wipe her face.

"I thought you quit work."

She turned, beginning to get angry all over again at his accusatory tone. "I quit my jobs," she corrected. *He's grieving. Remember that.* "Millinery is my work."

"Hats." He sounded dubious. Picking up a piece

of black netting, he arched an eyebrow. "You add frills and feathers?"

"I make one-of-a-kind hats and matching handbags." She picked up a framed citation from the Smithsonian thanking her for her work in assisting with a Confederate headgear restoration. "I also contract to work on special projects and I've been asked to put together a book, an overview of hats through the ages."

"Wow. I'm impressed." He sounded sincere, but she'd been taken in before by his seeming civility before he'd shredded her with unkind words again, so all she did was eye him dubiously.

"I am," he said. "How did you get so knowledgeable about hats?"

"I told you before that I was fascinated by hats when I was young."

He nodded.

"My mother encouraged my interest and helped me acquire a sizable collection, which I donated to the Smithsonian last year. I also studied the history of fashion and millinery at college."

"Very impressive." Again he sounded as if he meant it. He fingered another stack of silk in various shades of blue. "Did Robin know you did this?"

She looked at him as if he were crazy, though the two simple words had made her pulse jump in a ridiculous way. "Of course. He was very encouraging."

"And you've never been here before? You didn't know he had this place in Maine?" His eyes were intent.

She shook her head, baffled by the apparent change of subject. "No. Why?"

"I think Robin remodeled this room for you," he said.

Garrett watched Ana's face. He hadn't really planned to blurt that out, but he'd just realized it and before he'd known it, the words were hanging in the air between them.

"What?" Her face was stricken, her voice incredulous.

"This room and the storage area next door were one big unfinished area until a year ago. When we were here last summer, Robin decided to put in a wall and divide the storage in two. He turned this one into a room he was calling his den. But he never used it. We always shared the downstairs office, and by the time this was finished, it was time to go back to Baltimore."

He looked at Ana closely. Her eyes were shiny and her nose was pink; she'd been crying when he came in. Crying over Robin? The thought annoyed him immensely, erasing the relaxed atmosphere.

He wasn't sure why the thought of her grieving for Robin got to him; it wasn't as if he had had a monopoly on his stepfather's attentions. But...the context in which he believed the woman had known Robin was still so offensive it made him want to throw up. How could she have let an old man's age-spotted hands run over that smooth alabaster flesh? How could Robin have let himself be blinded by her fresh, glowing face and stunning figure? God, he'd asked himself that question at least a million times in the past couple of days. Shouldn't the very thought that she was interested in a man so much older have been a red flag to his stepfather?

"Anyhow," he said, "I was planning to move my office up here."

Ana stood up, placing her hands on well-shaped hips. The action pulled her shirt taut against her breasts, flattening them slightly, and he could clearly see the outline of her nipples. It was hard to drag his gaze back to her face.

"This is a marvelous space for my work. I'm not switching. Especially if Robin created this with me in mind."

"We're sharing this place," he reminded her. He didn't really want the room so much as he wanted to let her know she was only there on sufferance. It was clear she was quite talented at the unusual career she'd chosen, although it didn't sound as if it brought in much income.

"That's exactly right," Ana said. "You have a bedroom, I have a bedroom. You have a workroom, I have a workroom. You chose yours first, I just took what was still vacant. I plan to work in here and if you want it, we can fight for it." She paused for breath and looked around the room, and when she spoke again, her voice was less strident. "Robin would be thrilled that I'm using it."

"Oh, and you're the expert on what Robin would have wanted."

"No." She seemed to deflate before his eyes. "You had him for nearly two decades. I'm sure you know many, many things about him that I don't.'' She turned away and began to fiddle with small boxes of gems and sequins, aimlessly arranging and rearranging them.

''So you're pretty good at this,'' he said, letting it drop. He eyed the Smithsonian citation. She must be better than good; she must be *excellent*.

She didn't answer him.

''Are you?''

Ana stopped. ''Robin thought I was,'' she said in a small voice. ''I'm sure that's why he made this provision for me. He wanted me to have the time to work without having to worry about making ends meet.''

''Well, you've certainly managed that,'' he said, anger rising again. ''And when I buy out your share of this place, I have no doubt that I'll be paying three times the market share.''

''I told you before that I'm not selling.'' Her eyes had narrowed and the hesitancy he'd sensed had fled.

''We'll see.'' He sneered. ''I've met women like you before.'' As he turned and strode out the door, all he could see was a woman who had wanted a man for his money. And unlike his dear, departed fiancée Kammy, Ana had managed to get what she wanted.

She started her campaign to take him down a few pegs the next day at lunchtime. So what if he was grieving? He'd been a perfect ogre last night and he deserved everything he got, she thought, still smarting from his last comments.

She'd had breakfast at seven-thirty, despite the fact

that waiting so long after rising at six and swimming made her feel faintly nauseous, because Garrett the Grinch had the kitchen from six-thirty until seven-thirty.

Then she had to turn around and have her lunch hour beginning at eleven-thirty because he got the kitchen at twelve-thirty. She was quietly steaming and ready for action when she stopped for the morning.

The first thing she did was boil the chicken while she assembled the ingredients and mixed together the rest of her casserole ingredients. Next she mixed up a generous amount of crab dip with the meat she'd bought when she ran to town a few hours ago. Living along the coast had its advantages, she decided as she popped a bite of the succulent Dungeness crab into her mouth.

Ordinarily she would have let the chicken cool before picking and chopping it into small chunks, but because of the time constraint, she had to do it as soon as it was done cooking.

The fact that she burned her fingertips was another black mark against Garrett's name.

It was 12:25 when she finally got the chicken mixed into the casserole with the broccoli, cream sauce, mushrooms and herbs. She liberally topped it with cheese and crumbled breadcrumbs then popped it into the preheated oven just as Garrett walked in the door.

He made a production of checking his watch. "Am I early? I don't want to rush you out of the kitchen."

She smiled as graciously as she could manage, buoyed by the thought of what was going to happen in the next hour. "No, I was just finishing. I hope you don't mind—I left a casserole in the oven to bake."

He shrugged. "I wasn't planning on using the oven. Feel free."

"Thank you." She shaded her voice with just a touch too much gratitude. "I'll be back to get it out but you'll be almost done in the kitchen by then." She turned to the counter and picked up the plate of crab and crackers she'd set out.

"What's that?" he asked.

"A little crab dip I mixed up," she said airily. "I have a fabulous recipe."

As he watched, she turned away and headed for the door. "Since it's your kitchen time, I'll take myself out onto the deck. After that, I'm going to take the canoe out for a little while." She smiled to herself, imagining him drooling.

To her surprise, Garrett trailed after her. "Do you wear a life vest when you go out alone?"

She shook her head. "No. I'm quite a strong swimmer." Then she smiled. "Don't worry. I won't drown before the month is up and we own the cottage."

He shot her a look of annoyance. "Water safety is nothing to be flippant about. You should be wearing a vest." He paused. "Actually, you shouldn't be going out alone at all."

That surprised her. No, that *shocked* her. Anger began to simmer. "You do."

He frowned. "That's different."

"Oh?" She made her voice mocking. "Because

you're a big, strong man and I'm just a silly little woman who needs taking care of?''

"No." His eyes were growing dark and stormy. "Because I've been coming here for years and I'm familiar with the lake and you're not. There are some dangerous rocky areas out there. And unlike most of the lakes, this one isn't so heavily populated that you'd be rescued anytime soon. Even if you didn't hurt yourself and drown, you might have to wait there until I missed you."

"Goodness, that *could* take a while," she said acidly. "Since we both know how likely it is that you'd miss me for anything other than a convenient target for your rotten temper."

His face was growing red; he looked furious. "Are you going to be sensible or not?"

She smiled and waggled her fingers at him as she stepped out onto the deck. "Not."

Four

He woke up in a bad mood.

As Garrett swung his feet over the edge of the bed and stood, he heard a raucous squeak, then the quieter *snick* of the kitchen screen door latching. He stopped in mid-stretch and glanced at the clock. Six-thirty. That meant that the sound he heard must be Ana coming in from her swim. He told himself he wasn't disappointed that he hadn't risen early enough to see her emerge from the lake. But a part of him could still visualize the perfect, slender limbs, the full breasts and rounded hips and his body called him a liar.

What was the matter with him, lusting after a woman who had probably slept with his stepfather? He was afraid he knew exactly what was wrong with him. The luscious Miss Birch was intensely attractive, immensely sexually compelling. The same thing that had worked on Robin was working on him, as well.

The thought made him want to snarl as he shrugged into a T-shirt, shorts and dockside shoes before heading downstairs. Why had men been made this way? It wasn't that he liked *her,* he assured himself. It was just that she was so incredibly well put together. As he entered the kitchen, he wondered where she had gone—but his question was answered when he saw her standing at the counter spreading butter and jelly on two slices of toast.

"Good morning." He forced himself to be civil.

"Good morning." She sent him a beaming smile. She wore a long beach wrap that clung to her wet body and her hair was wrapped turban-style in a towel. She wasn't wearing a scrap of makeup but his gut clenched as the potent impact of her shining beauty hit him. Life just wasn't fair.

"It's past six-thirty," he said abruptly. "My time in the kitchen."

Ana gave a gusty sigh and the smile faded. "Oh, heavens, please excuse me. God forbid I should be in the kitchen during *your time.*" Her voice dripped with sarcasm.

It fed his general discontented feeling and he shot her a glare. "We made a deal. The deal is you're out of the kitchen when it's my turn. You can eat before or after, whichever you choose."

"Before or after doesn't work well for me." She picked up her toast and placed it on a plate, then poured herself a glass of orange juice. "I'm starving.

I can't wait until seven-thirty to put something in my stomach or I feel ill.''

"Six-thirty to seven-thirty is my kitchen time," he said stubbornly. "You get up at six. Eat before you swim."

"I can't. It's not good to exercise on a full stomach."

"So swim later in the day."

"I don't *want* to! I like to exercise first thing in the morning. If I get caught up in a project I'll forget if I leave it until later." She unwrapped the towel from her hair and began to comb her fingers through the wild tangle of irrepressible curls. "Who in the world needs an hour to eat breakfast, anyway? It's not like you make a gourmet meal. You eat *cereal*."

"I read the paper. Drink my coffee."

"And you couldn't do that in the living room?" She sniffed as she picked up her dishes and started out of the kitchen. "Admit it. You're still mad about me inheriting half of this cottage and you're taking it out on me. *Robin's* the one you should blame."

"Robin's not the one who wormed his way into an old man's will." The moment the words left his mouth, he regretted them. Not because they weren't true, but because he really hadn't wanted to push Ana into a state of war. Life in the little house was difficult enough.

Ana whirled. Her exercise-pinkened face had grown pale, except for two spots of color high on her cheekbones, and she was practically shaking with anger. "For your information, Robin is the one who sought me out. After we met, I never asked him for anything except the pleasure of his company.''

She stomped out of the kitchen. Her cat, Roadkill—what kind of a name was that to stick an animal with?—darted after her, pausing in the doorway to whirl and hiss at him with a sobering display of fangs. He'd heard cat bites were extremely painful and often got infected. That animal was dangerous. He should demand that she keep it penned up or get rid of it.

He took every minute of the rest of his hour to read every inch of the paper that the caretakers delivered just after dawn. When he got his milk and orange juice out of the refrigerator, he couldn't help but notice the casserole she'd made yesterday afternoon. It didn't look like much, just a baking dish with a crumb-covered cheese crust inside. But the smell of the thing while it was baking had practically had him drooling. He wondered if he could get her to give him the recipe to take home to his cook. Then, remembering the harsh words they'd just exchanged, he decided he'd be a fool to ask. She'd probably give him a recipe for something poisonous.

He went down to the lake and took a good swim as Ana had earlier. But when he came back to the house and settled in his office, the mood of restless discontent still rode him. He checked his watch. Eight-forty. His New York office didn't open until nine and L.A. was three hours behind that. While he knew he paid his staff generously enough that he could call one of them at home, he refrained. He tried never to infringe on his employees' downtime except when truly necessary. Today it wasn't.

Rising from his desk, he wandered through the kitchen into the living room.

Ana was standing on tiptoe at the door with a small bottle of oil in one hand, stretching up to reach the top hinge. Guilt struck immediately. He'd been inexcusably rude. And worse than that, just plain mean. He shifted uncomfortably as another truth struck home: *Robin would have been ashamed of him.*

A bolt of sorrow shot through him as, once again, he faced the fact that never again would he hear that voice, that laugh. And he remembered what Ana had said in the kitchen earlier. She'd never wanted anything but his company. Even as the cynic inside him said *right,* he realized that she also must be feeling a tremendous sense of loss. It made his voice less antagonistic, gentler, as he asked, "What are you doing?"

"Oiling these hinges," she said in a distinctly defensive tone. "Every door in this place squeaks. It was driving me crazy. I really want to be working, but I know I couldn't concentrate until I got this done."

He couldn't blame her, he decided as he walked over to stand beside her. He was the one who had started this. "How many have you done?"

"This is the last one downstairs except for the far door in the kitchen." She turned to look at him with lifted brows, and her green eyes were wary. "Why?"

He reached out and took the bottle from her. "I have a few minutes to kill until my offices open. Go ahead and work. I'll finish these."

Her face was so suspicious he would have been

insulted if he hadn't known full well he deserved her skepticism. "Really?"

Strangely, the seething anger with which he'd awoken seemed to melt away in that moment and he smiled. "Really."

Her whole face lit up. "Thank you!" And she dashed up the stairs without another word.

He oiled the remaining hinges downstairs, then went upstairs and methodically worked his way through the rooms. The last door he tackled was the door of her workroom. Just as he opened it to work the oil into one of the hinges, she pulled it open from the other side and barreled through.

She crashed straight into him, and they both staggered. Automatically he reached out and caught her by the shoulders, feeling the press of her soft skin beneath his palms. He let go of her instantly and stepped back. "Whoa. You all right?"

Ana stared up at him. She licked her lips. "Um, fine. Thank you," she added belatedly.

"No problem." He smiled at her, trying not to stare at her mouth as she nervously moistened her lips again, then felt the smile fade. "I, ah, owe you an apology for what I said earlier."

Her eyebrows lifted in that silent-but-oh-so-eloquent manner he'd come to recognize, but she didn't say anything.

"I...cared for Robin." He looked at the floor. "It's been difficult to adjust to the thought of sharing him with anyone, even in memory."

"I'm sure." She shifted beneath the weight of the backpack he'd just noticed she was wearing. "He talked about you all the time, you know. He was so proud of you. I don't think he ever thought about you not being his biological son. He—he loved you.''

Garrett stared at her. *Men don't cry,* he reminded himself fiercely. But he couldn't prevent the tight knot that rose in his throat and constricted his breathing, nor could he banish the tears that welled. He blinked them away, smiling crookedly. ''I loved him, too. He married my mother when I was a four-teen-year-old hell-raiser, and he took me in hand. I learned rules, and I learned manners. And somewhere along the way, I forgot that I didn't want to like this guy who'd invaded my life.''

Ana smiled. ''He was pretty irresistible.''

An awkward silence hung in the air as their eyes met and held. And held, and…held. Her green gaze was filled with sadness, warm fond memories and something more. Something that told him she was very aware of him as a man.

His pulse quickened. It was the first time he'd had any inkling that she was feeling the attraction he'd been fighting. And even though he told himself to ignore it, he wondered what she would do if he pulled her against him.

Then she broke the moment, giving him a wide berth as she stepped past him. ''I'm going to take a walk. I seem to think creatively when I'm walking. See you later.'' She paused. ''Thanks again for oiling the doors.'' The last was tossed over her shoulder as she rushed down the stairs.

Just as the door closed behind her, a movement from the corner of his eye distracted him. Turning his head, he was surprised to see that the cat had leaped up onto an end table and was peering out the window.

"I thought you were shut in her room," Garrett said softly.

The cat jerked its head and gave him what looked like a less-than-friendly feline stare.

"You fell into it and came up smelling like a rose," Garrett informed the animal. "I hope you know how lucky you are to have found a sucker like her." He took a step closer. Immediately the cat sprang to its feet. Though it didn't leap away, it was clear that he wasn't to be trusted.

"All right. I'll fix you," he murmured. Moving as slowly as he could, he backed away from the cat and went downstairs. In the pantry, on Ana's side, were stacks of canned cat food. He popped the top on one and forked half of the contents into a small bowl. After covering and refrigerating the other half, he carried the food back upstairs. The cat was still perched on the end table.

"Hey, cat, I'm back. And do I have a treat for you." He eased as close as he dared, watching the cat's muscles tense. He kept talking in a soft, soothing tone as he extended the bowl and set it on the floor not far from the animal. The cat's nose was twitching. "Go ahead, dig in," Garrett invited. "See what a good guy I am?"

The cat continued to eye him mistrustfully as he backed away. Then, once the animal judged him to be less of a threat, it leaped down from the table and attacked the food with gusto, glancing up occasionally to make sure Garrett hadn't invaded its personal space.

"Good stuff, huh?" He watched as the cat cleaned the bowl with vigorous strokes of its tongue until it appeared as clean as it had been before he'd put food in it. Only the fishy smell still lingered.

When the cat finished eating, it sat and began to clean itself with delicate swipes of one striped paw. "You really are a beauty," Garrett murmured. And it was. It was, as he'd deduced the first night he'd glimpsed it, a pretty tiger-striped tabby. But instead of plain stripes, the bands of contrasting color whorled into a perfectly round bull's-eye pattern on each side.

He took a step closer, and then another when the cat ignored him. He crouched and snagged the bowl, and the cat looked up. He extended his hand. "Hi." The cat sniffed his hand, finger by finger, for a very long time. Then, just as he knew he was going to have to get up before he lost all feeling in his legs, the animal stretched forward and butted its head against his hand. He turned his hand over slowly and gently scratched behind its ears. A loud rumble filled the room as the cat began to purr, the noise sounding like a poorly-tuned outboard motor.

"Well, I'll be damned," Garrett murmured. "You big faker." He moved his hand away and began to rise. The cat shot him one wild-eyed look, laid its ears back and hissed, then vanished into Ana's room.

Garrett chuckled. He shrugged as he picked up the bowl and carried it downstairs. "Oh, well. Small steps are better than none."

It was past time for his offices to be open, so he headed for his study and worked for the rest of the morning. Around eleven he smelled something delicious, something like…cherry pie? It was a good thing Ana didn't know what the smell of her cooking was doing to him or she'd have a good laugh at his expense, he thought as he forced himself to ignore the odor. At twelve-thirty, his watch alarm reminded him that it was lunchtime, a fact his stomach already knew, and he finished his last conference call and went into the kitchen.

Ana stood by the counter, lifting the casserole she'd made out of the refrigerator and setting it into an oversize picnic basket he'd seen in the pantry. Her curly hair was caught in a loose ponytail at her nape and wild quirky strands formed a halo around her head. She wore an ivory sundress, a gauzy thing with a fitted bodice and gathers down the front that gave the skirt additional fullness.

"Hello," she said, placing a wooden thing that looked like a miniature table into the basket with its legs on either sides of the casserole dish.

"Hello." He eyed the basket. "Going on a picnic?"

She shook her head. "No. Taking a few little things to a friend in town." She turned from him and lifted a pie from the counter, setting it on the second shelf she'd made of the little wooden thing.

He couldn't help himself. "Is that cherry pie?" He sniffed appreciatively. Hopefully.

"Yes." She snapped shut the basket lid and swung the basket down from the counter, and he could see the play of smooth muscle in her arms as she absorbed the weight. "I'm having dinner in town so you won't have to worry about me infringing on your kitchen time tonight. See you later."

"See you later," he echoed stupidly as she whisked around him and out the back door. As she started up the hill, he had to restrain himself from charging after her and demanding, "Dinner with who?"

It's none of your business, he admonished himself. As if he didn't know what she'd say if he were to do something so stupid.

She still hadn't returned by the time he'd cleaned up the dishes from his solitary meal that evening. The peace and quiet was kind of nice, he told himself stoutly. He'd never been up here without Robin, never had to eat his every meal alone. There was absolutely nothing wrong with it. Absolutely nothing.

He decided to do a little fishing, so he cut up some bait and took the canoe to the far southern end of the lake where he knew there was a good small-mouth bass hole. After an hour and a half, he'd caught three fish—more than enough for dinner the next evening—and dark was falling. It was peaceful and pretty on the lake as the light dimmed and the sky moved through pinks and lavenders to indigo and finally black. The loons hooted insanely as they prepared to settle in for the night.

As he paddled leisurely back toward the cottage, he realized there was a light on in the living room. He'd turned it off, he was sure, because the only light he'd intentionally left on, the one by the door, was still shining, a beacon beckoning to him.

Ana must be home. His pulse sped up and there was a surprising sense of anticipation churning in his belly. He hauled the canoe out of the water and stowed the paddles and life vests, then lifted his string of fish and strode up the steep trail through the pines and the birches to the light.

The moment he stepped through the door he smelled popcorn. He inhaled deeply, reflexively, as he took the fish to the kitchen.

"Hello," Ana called as he flipped on the light above the sink.

"Hi." Then he remembered she'd had dinner with someone, somewhere. "Have a nice evening?"

"Marvelous," she said in a cheery, breezy tone, and he wondered who she'd been with to put that note of happiness into her voice. He couldn't think of any way to ask her without risking another angry exchange. And though he'd started the hostilities, he found he didn't really want to fight with her anymore. It took too much energy, all negative.

The sound of the television show she was watching penetrated his consciousness as he was washing his hands after finishing cleaning the fish. "Hey," he said, moving into the living room. "I didn't think about the television. We're going to have to set up a viewing schedule, I guess."

Ana glanced at him, and he saw her shake her head in resignation, smiling wryly. "All right," she said. "I get tonight. And Monday. Anything else is negotiable."

"But tonight's Thursday." He shook his head. "I

like the Thursday night lineup on NBC. And there are a couple of shows I enjoy on Monday night, too.''

"So do I.'' Her eyebrows rose and there was a challenging look in her eyes. "And I was here first.''

He thought for a moment. "We could flip for it.''

"Not a chance.'' She dismissed him and turned back to the television. "But I'm willing to share with you. Think we could spend time in the same room without coming to blows?''

He snorted, well aware that he'd been the unreasonable one right from the start. "I guess we could try it and see.'' He dropped down on the sofa at an angle to the easy chair in which she sat. "I'll even let you sit in my chair.''

"Gee, thanks,'' she said dryly. "You're too kind.'' Then she uncurled her legs from where she'd tucked them up beneath her. "I'm going to make some more popcorn. Want some?''

He looked up at her. She'd lit the fire and at the moment, she was standing directly between him and it. Her thin, gauzy dress was sheer enough that with the light behind her, he could see the soft curves of her body. "Oh, yeah,'' he said. "I want some.''

Ana blinked. Two vertical lines appeared between her brows as she processed the response, as if she thought he might have meant something more than simply popcorn. Then she shrugged. "Okay. I'll be right back.'' She turned and whirled out of the room, the dress flowing around her, and he was reminded suddenly of a fairy, or a sprite. Not a typical thought for him, but then again, there was little typical about the way Ana had affected his life.

She was as good as her word and in a minute she returned, bearing not just a bowl of freshly buttered popcorn, but a drink for him. "I assume the beer in the refrigerator is yours," she said, smiling as she handed him the can, "since it isn't mine."

"You assume correctly. Thank you." He popped the top on the beer and took a long, cold drink, then stretched out his hand in her direction. "May I have the remote, please?"

Ana made no move to hand it over. "This remote?" She held it up. "You mean the one that controls the channels?"

"That's the one."

"How do I know you aren't planning a devious channel-changing operation the minute I hand it over?"

He had to chuckle. "A devious channel-changing operation? Nothing so impressive. It's just a guy thing—I feel incomplete without that remote in my possession."

Ana's gaze met his, and then she laughed aloud. "Now *that* explanation I believe. You know," she said and he noticed she still didn't hand over the little box, "I truly can't believe that a man with as much money as you have—or Robin, for that matter—wouldn't have more than one television in this place."

"It's called a cottage for a reason." He tossed a piece of popcorn into the air and caught it neatly in his mouth.

"I suppose you're right." Her eyes lit up, a glowing sea-green in the flickering light of the fire. She smiled warmly at him.

He felt his own lips pulling into a smile as he gazed into her eyes. There was a pleasant stirring of arousal lightly flirting with his senses. He forced himself to look away from the lure of her smooth skin. "May I please have that?" He gestured for the television remote control she was holding.

She was still laughing at him. "Going into withdrawal?"

"Yeah. Am I looking peaked?"

"Good try." But she handed it to him. "Here. I just hope you're not one of those frantic button-pushers who has to check ten other channels on every commercial break."

He held his tongue.

She groaned. "Oh, no. You *are*."

He had to chuckle again. "Relax. I'll be a perfect remote handler, I promise. So what other shows do you watch in the evening?"

Comparing their tastes, they found that they both watched a few select shows on Monday, Wednesday and Thursday. The rest of the week, neither really cared whether or not they even turned it on.

"Except for the financial news," he amended. "I like to keep track of the stock market."

She wrinkled her nose. "Be my guest. I check out the headlines and the weather channel and that's it."

He finished his beer and emptied the popcorn bowl after she said she was full. Her cat wandered in a short time later and licked the butter off the bowl, then hopped up into Ana's lap. It gave him one beady-eyed glare, apparently forgetting that he'd been the bearer of food just that morning, then completely ignored him.

"She's getting a lot friendlier," Ana commented. "When I first brought her home I couldn't even touch her. She hid under the bed all day and came out at night to eat."

"So how did you get her to come to you?"

She grinned, and the mischievous expression tightened his gut in a manner that had nothing to do with amusement. "I withheld her food until she came out after it. After about two weeks of that, she let me touch her."

"And you've had her how long?"

"Four months."

He was impressed with himself. He'd touched the cat practically the first time he'd made any effort. Then again, Ana had already done the hardest work of socializing the animal.

They shared laughter during two particularly funny sitcoms. The one-hour drama from ten to eleven was as intense as it ever had been, and he caught her wiping tears when a young boy died. She had a tender heart, he thought, watching the way the cat had curled up against her, its paws over her forearm as it purred loud enough for him to hear.

He'd probably purr, too, if she touched him like that, he thought, watching as her hand stroked steadily from the cat's head to its rump. The small action mesmerized him, and it wasn't until Ana said, "Would you like to hold her?" that he realized she had stopped watching the television and was watching him. The news had come on but he'd have been hard-pressed to tell anyone what the hot story of the day was.

"Uh, no." He could feel a dull flush sliding up his cheeks and he stood abruptly, grabbing the popcorn bowl and his beer and taking them out to the kitchen.

What the hell was wrong with him? He was *not* interested in Ana Birch. Well, okay, he wasn't going to lie to himself. The woman had a killer body, hair that made a man want to plunge his fingers into it and rub it against his skin, and the sweetest smile he'd seen in a long time. And she was nice. Really nice, unless she was a far better actress than he was giving her credit for. It was all too easy to see why Robin had fallen for her. And he must have, to have included her in his will.

The thought of Robin sobered him quickly. He couldn't reconcile the woman he was growing to know as warm, funny, and sunny-tempered when he wasn't provoking her, with the cold-blooded seductress that she would have to be to have seduced Robin for his money.

The two images simply wouldn't fit together and as she came into the kitchen with the cat weaving around her ankles to put her glass in the dishwasher, he muttered a good-night and escaped to his room.

Which one was the real Ana?

She was not going to fall for Garrett Holden.

She was *not* going to fall for Garrett Holden. A week later, Ana scrubbed the plate glass of the large living-room window that overlooked the lake with far more force than necessary. He was a bully and a brute and a mean, hateful person...but that hadn't been true for the five days since what she'd come to think of as The Television Truce. And if he smiled at her one more time and spoke to her in that deep, dark, honey-over-whiskey voice, she might just grab him by the hair and kiss him until this ridiculous fascination was slaked.

He wasn't playing fair, suddenly turning into an approachable, charming man.

She was *not* going to fall for him. At twenty-three, she'd had a number of relationships, though she couldn't say any of them had matured into love. The last one had been the longest: nine months. But she'd ended it a year ago when he'd made it clear he considered her millinery aspirations a little hobby that she probably wouldn't have time for once marriage and children came along. She sniffed, recalling the stupefaction on Bradley's face when she'd given him his walking papers. He truly hadn't understood.

But she had. Her mother had loved only one man in her whole life: Robin Underwood. And though Janette had been the one to leave and had never gone back, Ana had grown up knowing that such an all-consuming love was both powerful and possible. Maybe that was why she'd never had her heart broken. She was, perhaps subconsciously, looking for that kind of feeling.

But she'd never imagined that one person could feel such a love without the other reciprocating. She didn't love Garrett that way. *Yet.* Instinctively she sensed that he could break her heart without even trying. He—

"Good morning."

She jumped at least a foot in the air and the hand holding the wet rag sloshed a long, dripping streak across the newly cleaned window. Turning, she saw the object of her thoughts standing in the door to the kitchen.

His chest was heaving and he wore nothing but brief jogging shorts and footwear. His big body was as hard and sculpted as anything she'd imagined, and he glistened with sweat.

It took every ounce of willpower she had not to go to him and trace her hands over all that bare, tanned flesh. "Good morning," she said, hoping her voice didn't betray her state of nerves. "You scared me."

"Sorry. I was out running." He paused. "What are you doing?"

"Washing the windows." Wasn't it obvious? "I took down the drapes and threw them in the washer. When they're done I'll hang them out back and we'll have a nice, fresh-smelling room tonight."

Garrett was frowning. Good. She was used to his frowns. "We can hire someone to do more heavy-duty cleaning, if you like. You shouldn't be doing that."

She stood and stretched her back. "Why not?" Then she realized that the position she'd taken, with her palms behind her massaging the base of her spine, thrust her breasts forward in a way that probably seemed like an invitation. Garrett had noticed; his gaze had strayed from her face to her body and she saw him swallow. The betraying motion sent a shiver of sensual heat through her and she had to catch her breath. She was *not* falling for him, she reminded herself as she quickly lowered her hands and crossed her arms.

She could almost see him forcing himself back to the conversation. He spread his hands, clearly searching for an answer. "I, uh, I don't know. If you think the place isn't clean I can have a word with the Davenports—"

"Don't you dare!" She let her exasperation show. "They've done a wonderful job with routine maintenance and housekeeping. But every so often a house needs a thorough top-to-bottom cleaning. Like these windows, for instance. And the refrigerator and freezer should be defrosted and cleaned. The cushion covers on the furniture should be washed or dry-cleaned and the traps in the sinks should be—"

"Okay. I get it," he said. "We can hire someone younger and more energetic to do something like that."

She shook her head, smiling at him to soften her refusal. "No, 'we' can't. I can't begin to afford half of what that would cost. Don't worry, I don't expect you to do half the work. This is entirely voluntary."

"I thought you came up here to work on your hats and your book." He didn't sound angry; he was merely stating a fact.

"I can't work every minute," she told him. "Creativity just doesn't work like that. This kind of mindless work gives me a chance to recharge my battery."

"Does cooking serve the same function?"

"I guess so." She hadn't really thought about it before. "Yes. I sort of put my mind on automatic pilot when I'm cooking, too."

"Maybe we can make a deal," he said, and his eyes took on a crafty gleam. She could see his mind leaping ahead and she suddenly realized just how he'd parlayed an initial stock market windfall into a billion-dollar empire. "I'll pay for someone to do the housecleaning you want if you'll spend your creative downtime in the kitchen...*and* if you'll agree to let me share some of the product of your labor."

She stared at him, wanting to howl with laughter and knowing she'd better not. If Garrett thought she was pulling a fast one on him, they'd be back to armed warfare again. But still...men were so *easy* when it came to their stomachs. She'd hoped her cooking would get to him. Apparently she'd succeeded. "I suppose that would be okay," she said, drawing it out so that she sounded appropriately reluctant. Then she held up her hands, red and wrinkled from the morning's work. "My fingers will thank you."

Garrett smiled at her. Not a polite you-made-a-funny smile, but a warm, easy flash of teeth that scrambled every brain cell she had. Before she could regroup, he crossed the room, clasped her hands in his and drew her to her feet. "And my stomach will thank *you*." He didn't move away, simply held her hands between them in a loose clasp, looking down into her face.

His hands were hard and warm and she felt breathless, as if his proximity had stolen all the oxygen from the atmosphere around them. She was so close to his chest she could see the individual hairs that formed the curly mat across his breastbone, and he seemed to radiate an irresistible heat that enveloped her.

She felt tongue-tied, and abruptly flustered. Pulling her fingers free, she turned back to pick up the bucket and rags she'd been using. "I, uh, I guess I'll put these away and get to work now." She didn't glance at him as she carefully moved around him toward the kitchen door, but she was aware of the suspended quality of his stillness.

She emptied the bucket into the sink and rinsed it, then took the rags outside and draped them over the deck railing to dry. When she came back into the kitchen, Garrett stood beside the kitchen table, where she'd set a pile of old magazines she'd gathered up and set aside to throw out.

"Where did you find this?" His voice was sharp enough to make her jump. She turned in time to see him thump a finger on the top-most cover. It was a woman's issue, featuring exclusive makeup and hairstyles, thousand-dollar handbags and advice on how to make your mark at a society function.

"It was in the bathroom in that basket, I think. Who did this one belong to? It doesn't seem quite your style." She'd meant the comment to make him smile again, to be humorous since the other magazines all dealt with sports, finance or world news, but the moment he'd seen the magazine, the light had drained from his eyes, leaving a cool, expressionless mask that didn't reveal his thoughts.

"Toss it."

There was an awkward silence.

After a moment, she picked up the stack of magazines and started for the door. "All right."

"It belonged to my old girlfriend." His tone was almost grudging and with a flash of intuition she realized this was an uncomfortable topic for him.

She stopped in her tracks, turning slowly around though she didn't speak. His gaze met hers, and she was shocked to see raw pain in his face.

"She only came up here one time. It wasn't her thing," he said in a low voice.

He'd been hurt. Odd. She'd never thought of him as being vulnerable. Sympathy welled within her. "I'm sorry," she said, though he hadn't indicated there was anything wrong.

He shrugged. "Life happens. We move on."

They stared at each other across the space of the kitchen as his words echoed between them.

They did, indeed, move on. Guilt struck her. She needed to tell him who she was and why Robin had mentioned her in his will. Now she regretted that she hadn't done so sooner, regardless of his attitude.

But before she could speak, he said, "Would you eat dinner with me tonight? I hate eating alone." His voice was plaintive and she smiled.

"I thought you wanted it that way."

His answering smile was wry. "So did I. But it's lonely. Robin wanted us to share this place and I haven't done a very good job of honoring his wishes."

Tell him! urged the voice in her head.

But as she gazed into the sapphire depths of his

eyes, she simply couldn't open her mouth. The room was full of new, fragile feelings, feelings such as she'd never experienced before, and she couldn't bring herself to ruin the moment.

Soon, she promised herself. *I'll tell him soon.*

Five

Four more days passed. In a little over a week, the month would be over.

Nine days, and he would never have to see Ana again. The knowledge didn't delight Garrett as it might have a few weeks earlier. Tonight they'd had grilled steaks that she'd marinated all day and he'd done on the grill. They'd worked together chopping up a salad with an ease that he found far too appealing.

He stepped through the sliding door and walked down the steps from the deck to the path that led to the beach. As he picked up his fishing gear and eyed the setting sun, his gaze automatically swept the area.

Ana was in the same spot she often was at this time of day, relaxing on a chair she'd dragged down from the deck, her sketch pad in her lap.

"Hi," he said, pausing as he passed her. "Any requests for tomorrow night's dinner?"

She tilted her head as if considering her answer, and he was distracted by the heavy fall of curls that swung across one shoulder. Without thinking, he reached out and pushed it back. His fingers slipped over the smooth, warm skin of her shoulder, bared by the sleeveless tank top she wore, and he couldn't prevent his index finger from extending itself and stroking a small pattern back and forth on the creamy flesh. God, she felt good!

"How about a few small-mouth bass?" Her voice sounded breathless, but it effectively broke into his most inappropriate thoughts about what he'd like to be doing to that skin.

Reluctantly he dragged his hand away. It was becoming all too easy to touch Ana. Bodies brushed in the kitchen, hands met over the remote control, and once or twice she'd asked for his help navigating the computer. He'd leaned over the chair behind her, trying desperately to resist the urge to bury his face in the wild, sweet-smelling curls of her hair and trying even more desperately to hang on to his common sense. Getting involved with her would be a huge mistake. Capital *H,* capital *M. Huge* Mistake.

"Would you like to come fishing with me?" Even as the question left his mouth, he was kicking himself. He didn't need to spend any more time around Ana. If anything, he should be spending less.

She'd set down her pencil and twisted around to look up at him, and her eyes were a vivid aqua in the late-day golden light. "I'll come if I don't have to touch the worms," she said.

The distaste in her elegant tones made him laugh. "I think I can save you from that. I'm using minnows for bait."

"Dead fish?" She shuddered and he chuckled again.

"I promise you won't have to deal with them." He paused. "Unless you want to."

She snorted and smiled. "Fat chance." She rose and he stepped back, waiting while she put away her things. Then they walked down the path to the little cove. He offered her his hand as she stepped into the canoe, trying not to notice how small and delicate her palm had felt in his, then untied the canoe, climbed into his end and settled down with a single paddle.

It was a beautiful evening. The last rays of the sun skipped across the lake and an eagle soared over their heads to its nest in the top of a tall tree. The craft cut easily through the smooth, calm waters toward the point where, years ago, he'd learned that the bass congregated.

"Robin taught me to fish," he said before he thought about the risks of introducing the older man into their easy silence.

But Ana only widened her eyes with an incredulous smile. "Really? I can't quite picture a man who seemed as suave and debonair as Robin in a sleeveless T-shirt working worms onto a hook."

He grinned at her reference to his attire. "There are those in the corporate world who couldn't imagine it of me, either. I guess we all have our little secrets.'' He looked over at her. ''What's your secret, Ana?''

She was trailing a hand through the water while he paddled. When she looked across the length of the canoe at him, he got the impression that she'd gone somewhere far away in her head, and the smile faded from her face. ''I'm illegitimate,'' she said.

She was what? He didn't know what he'd expected, but a bald confession like that definitely hadn't been it. He didn't know what to say. ''I'm sorry,'' didn't seem adequate. ''You were raised by your mother in England, weren't you?'' he said carefully. He'd suddenly discovered that he wanted to know about her. All about her.

Ana nodded. ''But I was born here. My father was American. My mother always told me he'd died before they could marry, but not long ago I found out he was still alive.''

''That must have been a shock. How did your mother explain that?''

''She didn't. Couldn't,'' she amended. ''She passed away when I was twenty.''

He was surprised. ''My mother died of a blood clot when she was sixty-six but your mother must have been a good bit younger than that. What happened?''

''Breast cancer.'' She drew out the words in her distinctive accent. ''She was only fifty-one. Far too young to die,'' she added quietly.

He nodded, letting the silence soothe them for a moment. Then he said, ''Did she really believe your father had died?''

''No.'' Her voice was quiet. ''It turns out he was

already married. Apparently she knew that from the beginning, but when she found out she was pregnant, she left him.''

"*She* left *him?*" he repeated. "That's not usually the way it happens."

Ana smiled slightly. "My mother wasn't a usual sort of woman. I imagine that she didn't want my father to feel pressured and she didn't want him to marry her simply because of me."

Some women in that situation, he reflected, would have been only too happy to use a pregnancy as a lever for marriage. It spoke highly of her mother's character that she'd made the difficult choice she had. "She must have wanted you very much, to have raised you alone," he offered.

She smiled and he could see the memories in her eyes. "She was my best friend."

"You were lucky." He cleared his throat. "My father met another woman and left when I was nine. It was an ugly, messy divorce."

"And then your mother met Robin?"

"Not until I was fourteen." He smiled, thinking back to those days. "By then, I'd turned into a seriously obnoxious little hoodlum. I bet Robin's heart sank the first time we met, although he was too nice ever to tell me."

"But you got along well with him, obviously," she said.

"Not at first." It wasn't something he liked to admit, but he felt the need to answer her honestly. "I was on the verge of becoming a true delinquent. Running with the wrong crowd, smoking, defying my mother, you name it. Robin stepped in and laid down the law as soon as we moved in with him. He insisted on meeting my friends' parents. He imposed curfews. He cut off my allowance until I started helping with chores and being polite to my mother. God, I hated him!'' he said with a laugh. ''But he made me settle down. I started paying attention to my grades because he paid me for each *A* I got. Robin was quite wealthy by most standards, and I liked the lifestyle, so I decided I'd better learn what I could from the old man.''

She looked startled. ''Did you call him that?''

''No, but that's how I thought of him. He was fifteen years older than my mother.''

''My father was seventeen years older than Mother,'' she said.

''Well, I didn't think of Robin as old for very long.'' He shook his head. ''He took me skiing and beat me down the damn hill every time. He taught me to fish, and to golf—''

''And to make money, apparently,'' she broke in with a mischievous smile.

''Well, yes,'' he admitted. ''He was pretty thrilled with my success.''

They were gliding into the grassy shallows along the point by now, and he slowly set down the anchor, then baited a hook and tossed it in. Ana didn't speak again, and he let the silence lie comfortably between them, amazingly content simply to be sitting there in a lazily rocking boat with her.

He caught three fish in less than half an hour, plenty for tomorrow's dinner for the two of them, and after retrieving the anchor, he began to pull for their cove. They were traveling against the current now and though it was calm, he had to put more effort into it than he had gliding along with the flow of water earlier.

"Brrr." Ana rubbed her bare arms. "It's getting brisk out here. I should know by now that I need a sweater in the evening."

"You can have mine," he said. He liked the mental image of her in his sweater, sleeves flopping well down over the ends of her arms, the soft fabric draping over her breasts—

"That's all right. We'll be back in a minute."

But he rose to his knees anyway and began to strip the sweater over his head. The boat drifted for a moment as he did so, and just as he pulled his arms out of the sleeves, he heard Ana say, "Oh, no!"

And that fast, they were in the water.

It was *cold.* He sank beneath the surface and came up kicking. "Ana!" he yelled as soon as he could drag air into his lungs.

"I'm right here," she said immediately. "I'm fine." He relaxed as he heard the laughter in her voice. "But this water is *freezing."*

"What the hell happened?" he asked. They were treading water, and he looked around, grabbing the boat before it could get away. Ana swam around and collected life preservers and the blue-and-white cooler in which they'd stashed the fish.

"Well," she said in a surprised tone that made him start to laugh. "I do believe it was my fault. You were taking off your sweater and I turned around to get the cooler from the front since we were getting close to the dock. I must have leaned a little too far over on the same side you had most of your weight on—your *considerable* weight on—and the next thing I knew, we went bottom up.''

He was still laughing. ''There's no point in trying to get back into the canoe. It would take us longer than it will just to swim in.''

She agreed, and they set off, side by side, herding their respective items in front of them until they reached the dock. In the shallower water, he was able to stand, and he flipped the canoe upright again, then tied it at the end of the dock. She was already up the ladder when he hauled himself onto the dock and they stood there looking at each other, grinning like idiots.

''If Robin could see us now...'' she said.

''I think he can.'' He wanted to believe it. ''He's probably rolling around on what passes for the floor of Heaven, laughing at us.''

She smiled at him, shaking her head and lifting her hands to wring the water from the mass of her hair.

How could she be so beautiful, soaking wet? The sun was almost gone now but he could still see her clearly. There was something ineffably feminine in her movements, the graceful bow of her back as she bent at the waist, her vulnerable nape as her lifted arms pulled her hair forward and wrung out the excess water. He wanted to kiss her there, right on that exposed spot. He wanted to nuzzle beneath her hair and nibble on her neck, to take her face in his hands and lift it for his kiss.

He took a deep, unsteady breath, conscious of his racing pulse. This wasn't right. And then Ana straightened. The dripping tank shirt clung to every curve, and though she wore a bra, he could see that her nipples had drawn into tight little points. God, he thought, it wasn't fair. How could he be expected to resist her?

He dragged his gaze up to her face. Her mouth was slightly open, her color high. Then their eyes met—

And he was lost.

"Ana." He breathed her name as he took a step forward and pulled her into his arms. She made a startled sound, and her palms came up against his chest, but she didn't pull away.

They stared at each other for a long, suspended moment. Her gaze didn't move from his and he could see in her eyes the exact instant when she accepted the inevitable. Her pupils dilated and her shallow breathing echoed his as he said her name again.

"Ana."

Then he slowly lowered his head.

She sucked in a sharp breath, almost a gasp, as his lips settled over hers, and a sound like a small moan came from her throat. Her fingers dug into the pads of muscle on his chest but he barely noticed the small pain. All he noticed was her.

Beneath his mouth, her lips were soft. So soft. They moved willingly beneath his, clinging as he changed the angle of the kiss.

His hands were on her back, and he slowly rubbed one palm up to her nape and settled it beneath the wet mass of her hair, directly on that tender, sweet skin he'd been fantasizing about only a moment ago. Her hands and arms relaxed and she slid them up around his neck, her small fingers caressing his skin as she pulled his head more firmly down to hers. The motion left a cold, empty space between them and without thinking he tightened his grip on her and slid one hand down her back, drawing her against his hard, aching body.

The feel of her firm, gentle curves made his breath shudder out in a ragged cadence. Her gently rounded breasts flattened against his chest and her soft thighs cradled his. He felt arousal rush through him, felt her body firmly pillow his rapidly hardening flesh, felt the involuntary shiver that arched her silently against him, increasing the pressure in his loins and tantalizing him with the sweet shift of her hips moving over his. It was such an exquisite sensation that a deep growl of frustrated delight rose in his throat—

And in an instant, she wrenched herself out of his embrace. Her hands flew to her cheeks. "Oh, heavens!" she said. "This was a mistake!" And before he could form even the beginnings of a coherent thought, she spun and raced up the path to the cottage as fast as she dared to move over the uneven path.

He stood where he was, looking after her until she vanished inside the door. *What had he been thinking?* As he trudged up the slope with the fish cooler, he decided it wasn't a question of what he'd been thinking, but one of why he *hadn't* been.

He could hear the water running in the shower when he got inside. After he gutted and cleaned the fish and refrigerated them for tomorrow, he changed into dry clothes. He built up the fire while he waited for her to come out, all the while trying to decide what he was going to say to her. But before he was ready, before he'd figured it out, he heard her coming down the stairs.

He popped up from the couch where he'd been sitting and rushed into speech before she'd even reached the bottom of the steps. "You were right when you said it was a mistake. Please accept my apology." He shrugged, trying to lighten the tension. "It seemed like the thing to do at the time."

Something changed in her eyes, as if a door closed in his face. "Apology accepted." She never even broke her stride, merely continued through the room and on into the kitchen, effectively dismissing him.

He opened his mouth, about to go after her and protest, about to tell her...tell her what?

That he wanted to make love to her more than he'd wanted anything in years?

That he couldn't keep his eyes off her beautiful body, couldn't keep his mind off the intriguing puzzle that she was?

What he needed wasn't her so much as it was a woman. Any woman. He'd never been big on short-term indiscriminate sex, so he tended to go without while he was between relationships. Which he was now, and had been for too long to bear thinking about.

He reviewed the few women whose acquaintance he'd made over the years he and Robin had been coming up here. He'd gone out with one woman last summer a few times, and found her a pleasant enough companion, quite pretty, and though they'd never been intimate...he was pretty sure she wouldn't say no if he opened that particular door.

Good. He'd call her tomorrow. What was her name, anyway? Ellen? Elaine? No, Eileen. That was it.

He was almost positive.

Ana took a stuffed chicken and apple dumplings in to share with Teddy and Nola the next evening. As she took the meal from the oven, she wondered if Garrett was eating his bass. He'd been quiet and polite—and noticeably distant—all day. When she'd told him she was having dinner in town, he had grown very still for a long moment. Then he'd said, ''I guess you'll miss the fish. Sorry.''

While the meal baked, she and Nola had played Scrabble. She'd also talked Nola into letting her wash two loads of infant sheets, blankets and clothing and getting it all folded and put away while Nola supervised from a rocking chair. The young woman was growing larger by the day and it was becoming increasingly difficult for her to get around. Ana knew Teddy was worried. Nola's blood pressure had been higher than the doctor liked, he'd confided, and they were hoping the twins did come a little early. Sonograms showed both babies were a good size and appeared to be doing well.

She stayed to clean up after the meal and didn't get home until nearly eight. Garrett's car was gone when she pulled into their lane, and she told herself it didn't matter. She hadn't expected to see him.

Even if it was a Thursday and they always watched their shows together.

Immediately after that thought came an image out of nowhere. She sat on the couch with Garrett, cuddled into the curve of his arm. As the television show took a commercial break, he turned to her and sought her lips as she wrapped her arms around his strong back and pulled him down.... *Stop it, Ana Janette!*

Oh, how she wished she could. All day long she'd been trying not to think about The Kiss. All day long she'd had her brain invaded by the breathless, tingly sensation that accompanied any thought of the way he'd gently tugged her against him. His hand had played in her hair, his lips had been warm and firm and far too enticing. And when she'd stopped thinking and let herself go with the moment, sliding her arms up around his neck, he'd pulled her against him—against every muscled, hard, hot inch of him— and she'd nearly swooned in his arms with an overwhelming urge to drag him down to the dock and give herself to him.

It had been a shocking self-revelation, and she'd torn herself from his arms, angry with her yearning body and even more upset that her heart ached at least as much.

Too agitated to sit down and watch the television, she decided to take a run. She hadn't exercised today, other than swimming, so it would do her good. But as she established a steady pace, watching the rutted lane carefully for spots that might twist an ankle, her thoughts went right back to the evening before.

The time they'd shared on the lake had been lovely. Garrett had been friendlier and more open than ever. In fact, he'd been getting gradually more approachable all week. When he'd brought up Robin, she'd thought there might be an opportunity to tell him about her relationship, but he'd seemed to need to talk and she hadn't wanted to distract him…and she hadn't been able to bring herself to ruin the evening. She was a coward. It was as simple as that. If she'd confessed, she would have spoiled the perfect evening they'd been sharing, and lost the chance to learn more about Garrett.

And he'd never have kissed her.

Oh, that kiss. Thinking about it made her toes curl inside her sneakers.

Earlier, when he'd paused to talk and invited her to go out on the lake with him, he'd pushed her hair back and his hand had grazed her shoulder. He'd brushed his finger lightly but quite deliberately over her skin for a moment, and she'd had to catch herself before she reached up and laid her hand over his to hold the contact. Then he'd taken his hand away and she'd been sure he was sorry for letting himself touch her like that.

She'd been even more aware of him than ever out on the lake. She'd tried not to stare at the ripple of muscle in his bare arms as he rowed, tried not to notice the way the last rays of the sun had picked copper highlights out of his dark brown hair and turned them to fire, tried to keep her gaze from returning to the fascinating flex of his strong thighs as he braced for each stroke. She'd tried.

What a moment that had been on the dock, when she'd straightened up after wringing out her hair and caught him…wanting her. That was the only way to describe the look on his face as his gaze had traced a path down over her body, pausing at her breasts.

She had figured she probably looked like a candidate for a wet T-shirt contest and from the expression on his face, she'd been right. His naked need had shot out and enveloped her, making it impossible to move, to protest, to do anything but wait breathlessly as he pulled her into his arms.

And then he'd kissed her. She'd wanted it to last forever. Contrary to what she'd said, it hadn't *felt* like a mistake. It had felt like Heaven. It had felt *right*.

So why had she stopped him?

Because, she thought miserably, she hadn't been honest with him. And she knew him well enough to know that when she explained who she really was, there were going to be fireworks between them. And they wouldn't be the kind she'd welcome.

"Hello, dear!"

She shook her head as she waved at Mrs. Davenport, who was seated on her front porch. The older woman had a bowl in her lap and another on the floor, either shelling peas or snapping beans. Without even realizing what she was doing Ana had run all the way to the end of the lane. "Hello, Mrs. D," she called, slowing to a walk. "How are you this evening?

The caretaker's wife nodded. "Good," she said with the spare economy of a native of Maine. "You?"

Ana nodded. "I'm good. How could I be otherwise, up here in this lovely spot?"

"And with a handsome man like Mr. Garrett," the older woman said, a sly twinkle in her eye.

She hoped Mrs. Davenport wasn't a mind reader, Ana thought. The last thing she needed was for anyone to know how she was growing to feel about Garrett. "Having a handsome man around is always a bonus," she said lightly.

To her surprise, the woman's smile faded. "Don't you hurt that boy," she said. "That Kammy girl was bad enough."

"Kammy?" echoed Ana. "Do you mean the other woman Garrett brought up here? Because he and I aren't—"

But her words were lost on Mrs. Davenport. "Sneaky one, she was," the old lady muttered. She rocked faster, as if the chair were as agitated as she was. "Running around behind his back, all the while planning to marry him. I saw her meet her fella at the end of the lane. Kissing and carrying on something awful." She shook her head and repeated, "Sneaky one."

Running around behind his back...? Ana's sensitive heart shrank with pain. "But why...what kind of woman wouldn't want Garrett?" She stopped, conscious of the impropriety of discussing him with his employee, yet too shocked to hide her reaction.

Mrs. Davenport positively glowered, her normally pleasant countenance drawn into a fierce scowl. "After his money, she was. That's the story I heard from Mr. Robin." The rocking chair slowed its pace a fraction. "Burned him bad. You're the only one he's brought here since." She shook a finger at Ana. "So don't you hurt him now."

"No, ma'am." Desperate for a change of subject, Ana pointed at the bowl, which she could see was full of peas. "You got a good crop this year."

"It's been a good summer." Mrs. Davenport smiled, apparently dismissing the topic now that she'd said her piece.

After a few more moments of conversation, Ana said, "Well, I'd better get back."

Mrs. Davenport nodded. "I'm going in soon. The skeeters'll make a meal of you if you don't." She shot an odd, challenging glance at Ana. "Your mama always said those skeeters were big enough to carry her away."

"My...mother?" Ana felt like she'd been dumped into the lake. Icy fingers of shock dribbled down her spine. "You knew my mother?"

"I did." The elder woman's eyes assessed Ana's face. "Knew you were hers the minute I laid eyes on you."

"How...?" She stopped. The "how" was obvious. Robin had brought her mother here. "Robin brought my mother here," she said quietly.

Mrs. Davenport nodded. "The first time they came, 'tweren't nothin' but woods back there. They hiked back and looked around, and when they came out, Mr. Underwood bought it from us on the spot. Got the whole place built by the end of the summer, and the next summer, they spent the whole season up here. He had to go back down south a few times on business and she stayed here, but other than that, they hardly left." She smiled. "Never saw a couple so happy." Her smile faded. "But the next year, he came alone. I thought they'd get married, but she left him. Haven't ever seen her since."

Apparently the Davenports didn't know Robin already had been married when he'd brought Janette Birch to Maine. They'd adored him; telling them now would serve no purpose, so she merely said, "My mother's gone."

Mrs. Davenport's eyebrows rose. "I'm sorry for your loss." She hesitated, then set her peas aside and rose from the chair slowly. "Let me get a bag and you can take some of these peas along. We'll never eat 'em all."

Ana left to run back the lane a few moments later, a bag of green peas bouncing along in her hand. A peace offering of sorts, she imagined. And with every step, the shock of the caretaker's words vibrated through her anew.

Robin and her mother had come here together. Picked out the land and built the house. Together. And according to Mrs. Davenport, had spent the whole of the following summer here.

A fresh frisson shivered through her as the implications of that revelation struck her fully. She'd been born in early April…and very probably conceived right here in Eden Cottage the summer before.

Back at the house, she decided to wait until she had cooled down from the run before she showered. As she stowed the peas in the refrigerator, she bumped a container of lentil soup. It teetered on the edge of the shelf, then crashed to the floor, spilling soup across the kitchen. Muttering, she filled a bucket and began to scrub the kitchen floor. She was really going to need that shower, she thought ruefully. It was just as well Garrett wasn't home.

Garrett. She sat back on her heels, the scrub brush

motionless in her hand. She still found it hard to believe that any woman could prefer another man to him. Garrett was everything a woman could possibly want. Handsome, unquestionably. If she'd ever met a more attractive man, she couldn't remember when. Wealthy, yes, but in her book, wealth was definitely optional. Far more important, he had a sense of humor. He was intelligent and enjoyed a good argument. He definitely wasn't a man who thought women were a lesser species. And he was kind. A weird thing for her to think, given the way he'd treated her earlier in their…relationship. But though he didn't know it, she'd seen him with Roadkill, patiently talking to the skittish cat, slipping her treats, trying to win her affection.

Then that pesky *R* word surfaced again. Relationship. She and Garrett were not in a relationship, she reminded herself. Except one born of necessity and of the family connection about which he didn't even know yet.

Her heart sank, and she picked up the brush and dipped it in her bucket, then slopped a patch of soapy water over the floor and redoubled her scrubbing. She *had* to tell him about her father. Tomorrow. She would definitely tell him tomorrow, though she dreaded the thought. No man liked to look foolish, and she was very much afraid that's how Garrett would feel when he learned the truth. He might even think she'd kept it from him deliberately, that she'd been laughing at him for the past three weeks.

She hoped not. If nothing else, she hoped they could salvage the friendship from their relationship once he got over his anger. There was no one else who had known Robin like he did, and her lonely heart craved those shared memories almost as much as it did the other things Garrett could make her feel.

"Hello."

She bobbled her brush as someone behind her spoke. She wasn't sure whether it was fright or delight for a second, but the feeling of utter pleasure that hearing his voice provoked washed through her. She relaxed and her heart began to beat heavily, her reaction to him beyond her control. Garrett was back. And she knew what she had to do. She had to tell him. Right now, tonight.

She sat back on her heels, turning with a smile on her face. It froze in place when she realized he wasn't alone.

"Hello," she said uncertainly, looking from Garrett to the woman beside him.

The newcomer was blond. Very blond, and though it would have been nice to know it was a dye job, Ana suspected the color was real. It certainly highlighted her pale, porcelain skin and wide blue eyes well.

"Ana, this is Eileen." Garrett performed a perfunctory introduction. His gaze met hers and her heart contracted at the aloof expression on his face. As if he didn't care one bit what she thought.

And then she realized that he didn't. Why should he? She was the only one who was letting her heart get mixed into this mess Robin had forced on them. Unable to bear the distance between them, she transferred her gaze to his date.

"Welcome to Eden Cottage." Ana forced herself to smile at the other woman, though she could feel her cheeks burning.

"Thank you." The blonde's voice was clear and sweet.

Steadfastly, Ana kept her eyes on the other woman, refusing to look at Garrett again. The hurt rushing up inside her made her voice tight as she said, "I'm just finishing up here. I'll be out of your way in a minute."

"No rush," Garrett said. "We're going out on the deck." He took a bottle of wine from the counter, slipped a corkscrew into his pocket and pulled two fluted goblets from the cupboard.

He ushered his little blond beauty out of the room and she heard them pulling open the sliding glass door and stepping onto the deck.

Ana stood and carried the bucket to the sink to be emptied, then quickly mopped the floor with clean water. He was so *obvious*. Just like a man. Couldn't he have simply left things alone? After all, she was the one who had called a halt last night and pronounced their kiss a mistake. So why had he felt compelled to rub her nose in another woman's presence the very next evening? Did he think she was stupid? If he wanted to be sure they never got caught up in a moment like that again, all he had to do was say so.

A burning knot rose in her throat, and her chest felt as if it were being squeezed in a vise. She would *not* cry over him. She placed both hands on the edge of the sink and dropped her head, trying to control the feelings that wanted to burst out of her.

Oh, God, how had she come to this in three short weeks? The truth was, she didn't dislike or despise Garrett anymore.

She loved him.

Six

"I'll be back in a minute," Garrett said to his date.

"I'll be waiting," Eileen said coyly. She tossed him a smoldering look from her blue eyes and Garrett realized belatedly he was supposed to respond. But all he could manage to do was send her an abstracted smile as he stepped back into the house.

She hadn't been bad company. In fact, they'd had a very pleasant evening. He'd taken her to a restaurant high on a cliff overlooking Penobscot Bay and they'd enjoyed a bottle of local wine while they'd chatted. He'd found her as likable and pretty as he remembered. She also was a mathematics whiz, and she knew far more about the stock market than anyone would ever suspect. Still, he hadn't been attracted to her in any but the most generic way. When he'd invited her back to the cottage, he'd done so with the express purpose of letting Ana see that he had other fish on the line, that he didn't need her. Didn't want her.

But the moment he'd walked into the kitchen earlier, he'd known he'd made a mistake. One of monumental, only-a-man-would-do-something-so-dumb import.

Ana had been wearing a brief pair of yellow jogging shorts that showed her magnificent legs to advantage, and she must have gone running because she was still wearing her sneakers. The T-shirt she wore was liberally splashed with the water she was using to scrub the floor.

God. The last thing he needed was to be confronted with the sight of Ana in a wet T-shirt again.

Her hair had been carelessly twisted atop her head and stray curls fell down to wave around her face. She was working at a hot, messy job and her fine skin glowed with exertion. She should have looked like hell. Instead she looked as desirable as any woman in a sleek cocktail dress ever had looked to him.

She hadn't heard them come in, and for the barest moment before she'd registered Eileen's presence, there had been something warm and welcoming in the private smile she'd begun to send him. Possibly even something intimate. He hadn't imagined it, of that he was absolutely positive.

But then she'd seen his date. The smile froze, then disappeared. The expressions that rushed across her mobile features—shock, humiliation, and worst of all, unmistakable hurt—had been easy for him to read. The shock he'd expected. The humiliation he hadn't intended, but any woman caught scrubbing a floor when guests arrived would have felt the same. The hurt…how could he have known? he asked himself rather desperately. She'd made a point of rejecting him last night. She hadn't even stuck around to discuss what had happened, had simply dismissed it out of hand as a mistake, which had stuck in his side like a burr beneath a saddle. And so he'd decided to get a date, had taken a petty, juvenile action just because he wanted to show her that her words hadn't bothered him. A mistake, she'd said.

But the moment he'd seen her face tonight he knew she'd lied. For whatever reason, Ana hadn't wanted him to know how that kiss had affected her.

If it affected her anything like it affected me, we're in big trouble. If he had any sense, the last thing he'd be doing was going back inside to confront Ana. If he had any sense, he'd pretend he hadn't seen the raw emotion that had slipped out beneath her facade a few moments ago. If he had any sense, he'd lock himself in his room for the next few days and get the hell out of here on the thirty-second day without looking back.

But as he walked across the living room to the kitchen doorway, he knew he didn't have a single grain of common sense where Ana was concerned.

And then he saw her.

She stood in front of the sink, head down, with her elbows locked and her hands gripping the counter, as if she needed the support of her arms to hold her upright. There was defeat in her slumped posture, the way her weight rested on one leg. Even her curls seemed to have lost their spring.

"Ana," he said softly.

Her head jerked up and she whipped away, putting her back to him. But the one wild-eyed glance she'd shot in his direction had shown him clearly the tears brimming in her beautiful sea-green eyes. "Go away." Her voice was muffled; she hugged herself tightly with crossed arms.

"We have to talk," he said, as quietly as before. The urge to cross the room and take her in his arms was nearly irresistible but he forced himself to wait, sensing that she'd reject comfort—or anything else— right now. "Let me take Eileen home and then—"

"No," she said sharply. "I do *not* want to talk to you." Her voice was thick with distress and her back was rigid as she moved down the short hallway to the door. Before he could figure out what to say, how to handle this whole awful situation, she'd slipped through the door into the night beyond.

The *snicking* sound of the screen door latching galvanized him into action. Striding down the hall, he stepped out onto the porch, expecting that she'd be huddling there in the dark. It took a moment for his eyes to adjust, an especially long one because there was just the barest sliver of a new moon in the sky, but when they did, he realized the porch was empty.

Then he heard her footsteps on the path that led to their little beach. "Ana? Ana, wait."

The footsteps didn't slow. If anything, her pace increased. Garrett started to move as fast as he dared down the pebbled path, instinctively knowing what she intended. "Ana!" he shouted. "Don't go out on the lake. It's not safe."

Her footsteps thudding across the dock were the only answer he got, and he cursed vividly as he skidded on pine needles and nearly missed one of the rough rocks that served as steps. By the time he burst onto the dock, she was nothing but a dim blur moving rapidly away from the shore. Dammit! She knew he hated her going out alone. Now she was alone, on the lake, in the dark. His worst nightmare.

"At least wear a life jacket," he shouted after her.

"Garrett?" It was Eileen calling down from the deck where he'd left her. "I hate to break up the evening, but I need to get home soon." God, he'd forgotten all about her. Hell. Now he was stuck with her until Ana decided to come back in. No way was he leaving until he saw with his own eyes that she hadn't come to grief out there alone on the dark water.

"I can't leave," he said grimly. "It would be dangerous to leave while Ana's out on the lake alone."

Silence. He wondered if he sensed her surprise and rising suspicion, or if it were merely his conscience creating it in his head. Finally Eileen said, "She's a big girl," and there was the first touch of annoyance in her tone. "I suspect she's gone canoeing before without you to baby-sit."

He didn't bother to answer that, simply turned and stood at the edge of the deck, wishing to hell there was at least a little moonlight so that he could see where Ana had gone.

"I have to get going." Eileen tried again. "I have to work in the morning."

"I'm sure she'll be back soon," he said.

But Ana didn't come back soon. Half an hour

passed. He started to get concerned. What if something had happened to her out there on the pitch-dark water? Concern escalated into near-panic, and when Eileen said, "Calm down, Garrett. I'm sure she's fine," he realized he was pacing back and forth from one end of the deck to the other.

"Probably," he conceded. "But I still don't want to leave until she's out of the water."

His date cleared her throat. This time, when she spoke, there was a definite note of unhappiness. "Garrett, I really need to go home. Your roommate, or whatever she is, is being awfully inconsiderate, if you ask me." It was a blatant fishing expedition for an explanation.

"I didn't," he said between his teeth.

Eileen drew back with an affronted look on her face. "I beg your pardon?" she said in a frosty tone.

He dug his hand into his shorts' pocket and fished out his car keys. "Here," he said, tossing them at her. "Why don't you take my car? I'll get it tomorrow."

Eileen missed the keys. She bent to retrieve them, and as he watched her, he suddenly realized that when Ana made those same motions, it elicited a very different reaction. The sight of Ana's hair sweeping down, the bared, tender flesh of her nape, and the sweet curve of her bottom all turned him on. Totally, completely turned him on. As undeniably shapely as she was, when Eileen did it, it wasn't memorable in any way. At least not to him.

"Well, thank you," Eileen said in a voice that implied he deserved no thanks at all.

"I'm sorry this didn't turn out to be such a great evening." He knew he ought to at least go through the motions if he wanted to get this woman out of his hair without a scene.

"I'm sorry, too." From her tone, he surmised that he'd just been forgiven. She crossed to him and raised her arms to give him a brief hug. "If your... roommate moves out one of these days, give me a call again." She moved away then, a pretty woman sure of her appeal as her high heels tapped across the deck and around to the porch. "I'll leave your keys under the mat."

"Thanks," he said.

Thirty minutes later, Ana still hadn't returned. He was sitting on the deck nursing a beer, moodily reflecting on the past three weeks, when he heard the cat meow behind him. Actually it wasn't so much a meow as it was a squeak, and he wondered if its vocal cords had been damaged when it was hit.

Not it. She. It figured that Ana would have a female cat. Contrary critter. He turned and saw Roadkill sitting at the sliding door. "What's the matter, cat? Do you hate your name that much?"

The cat meowed again.

"I don't blame you," Garrett said. "I'd hate it, too. You deserve something prettier."

He'd slid shut the screen but had left the glass open and as he spoke, the cat raised one delicate paw and patted at the screen door.

"I can't let you out," he told her. "Ana would kill me if something happened to you." He looked down into his beer. "She probably wants to kill me, any-how."

The cat meowed a third time and patted the screen harder, and he heaved himself to his feet. "I'll feed you," he offered. "Maybe that'll take your mind off the great outdoors." The cat ran a few steps away when he went to the door, but to his surprise, she stayed close, meowing around his legs as he went to the kitchen and got out her food. The moment he set it down, she attacked it, and in minutes the bowl was licked clean.

"Good stuff, huh?" he asked her as she finally walked away from the bowl. She kept a wary eye on him as she sat and began to wash herself.

He might as well get his book, he decided, and read until Ana decided to come home. Ignoring the images of the canoe, overturned and empty, floating on the lake that assailed his imagination, he walked up the stairs. To his surprise, the cat came with him. He went into his bedroom and picked up the book he'd been reading from his bedside table, and she jumped up on his bed and daintily pranced across the quilt until she was close enough to touch.

"Tease," he told her. He slowly reached out his hand and her ears went back. He didn't move back but he stopped moving. They eyed each other. After a moment, she arched her head up beneath his hand, and he heard the ragged sound of her purring as he tentatively stroked her back. A ridiculous satisfaction leached through his tension. It was pretty pathetic when all it took to make him happier was one dopey cat.

She jumped down then, and went to the doorway, looking back over her shoulder as if she wanted him to follow her. He was going back downstairs anyway, so he snapped off the light and obliged. But she didn't go downstairs. The minute she saw him coming, she began to walk down the hallway, her tail held regally high, still purring like a poorly-tuned motorcycle. She went straight to the door of Ana's studio and disappeared inside—

Ana's studio! The door stood wide open. He knew she usually kept it closed because she didn't want the cat to get into any of the ribbon or lace that was all over the room. He knew because he'd checked a million times to see if the door was open and he could casually stroll by, maybe catch a glimpse of what she was working on. He'd seen very little of her work.

The door was open. The cat had gone in. He was going to have to go into her studio and get that cat. It wasn't snoopy; it was the act of a good… housemate? Roommate? Eileen had called her that, and her tone of voice had given the term a decidedly sexual meaning. His whole body tightened with a different kind of tension at the thought of sharing a room with Ana, of stripping away her clothing and baring that magnificent body, of laying her beneath him on his bed, of letting her masses of hair fall across his pillow.

He stood in the upstairs hallway and faced what he'd been avoiding for all these days, since the very first time he'd laid eyes on Ana. He wanted her. Not just the general wouldn't-it-be-nice kind of wanting, but a very specific I-have-to-have-*this*-woman kind of wanting. Even more than that, he was determined to have her. The kiss they'd shared could have started a fire in the kitchen and he knew instinctively that sex with her would be better than anything he'd ever known.

Had it been that way for Robin? The thought still pricked at him—at his pride?—but he was rapidly growing past caring that she'd been his stepfather's lover first.

If, indeed, she ever had been. Deep down, he couldn't reconcile the two images of Ana. The woman he was coming to know had integrity, honesty. She wouldn't have slept with an old man for his money. And though she'd undeniably known and loved Robin, he didn't get the sense that she was grieving for a lover.

But how else could she have known Robin? He knew for a fact that the only child Robin and his first wife had ever conceived had been stillborn. A son. The lack of children had been one of Robin's deepest regrets, and it spoke volumes about his integrity that he'd refused to divorce his first wife despite her obvious mental illness. No one would have blamed him, Garrett was sure. And after her death, he'd married Garrett's own mother Barbara, who at forty-nine was well past considering a pregnancy. Robin himself had been in his mid-sixties then, and his dream of children had died a quiet death years before.

No, Robin had no children. Otherwise, Garrett might have thought she was a grandchild. He tried to superimpose Ana's wild strawberry-blond ringlets and green eyes over the blue eyes and dark hair his stepfather had had in pictures he'd seen of Robin at a younger age, but he failed. The two looked nothing alike. Besides, he was sure Robin had had no other living relatives. They'd discussed it several years ago when Robin was drawing up his will naming Garrett his heir.

Nice try, he told himself. He was barking up the wrong tree, trying to come up with reasons, excuses, that would allow him to consummate this raging lust he felt for Ana without feeling too weird about the whole thing. Even he could see that.

Disgusted, he shook his head started down the hall. At the door of the studio, he stopped to flip on the lights, then blinked for a moment before moving forward. The light was bright. Very bright. He supposed that made sense for someone trying to work with color.

There were seven completed sets of hats and matching handbags laid out on the long counter along the wall. He studied each one, standing before them for long moments. He didn't know squat about women's fashions, but he did know that women wanted to look chic and expensive. And these accessories certainly looked to be both of those. They were good. *She* was good.

He'd known Robin must have thought she had talent, but discovering it for himself was another matter. No wonder Robin had wanted her to have time to pursue her craft!

The cat meowed, and he started for the door. But as he passed her big worktable, strewn with felts and fabrics, ribbons, feathers and other decorative items, he paused and stared.

The sketchbook she used to draw up rough drafts of her ideas lay open on the table. But there was no headgear displayed on the page. Instead a sophisticated sketch of a man's figure caught his eye. It was him! Himself? He? Whatever. The drawing showed him in profile, standing on the dock with his hands in his back pockets, eyes squinted as he looked out over the lake. He'd stood that way many times. And she'd noticed.

Curious, he flipped through a few of the other pages—and was struck dumb.

She'd drawn at least a dozen images of him. Standing, sitting. Sleeping, laughing. Close-ups and full-length views. It was extraordinarily odd to see himself drawn, though the sketches were so cleverly done that she'd made him look as if he were ready to step off the page.

Was there any significance to the fact that she'd drawn him? Or was it simply that he was the only person who was around on any regular basis? Why was she spending her time drawing a person at all?

The sound of the deck door sliding open and shut made him jump. Ana was finally back. Relief deeper than anything he'd ever experienced rushed through him; then he realized where he was. The last thing he wanted was for her to catch him snooping around in her studio, so he looked around for the cat. She was sitting atop a counter, washing herself again. He strode across the room and picked her up. "Come on, trouble. You don't belong in here."

Just as he stepped out of the room and turned back to close the door, Ana appeared on the stairs. Her eyes were huge, dark pools that looked bruised and weary in the harsh hall light and she hesitated when she saw him. He had the distinct impression she was about to flee again, but then she saw the cat in his arms. "You're holding Roadkill!"

Abruptly he realized that in his agitation he hadn't even thought about the cat's skittish nature.

Hastily he set her on the floor. "The door to your studio was wide open and she went in. I figured you probably didn't want her in there."

"Thank you." She was looking at the cat rather than at him, and she didn't appear to even have thought about the fact that he'd been in her workspace. "I could tell she was getting used to you but I can't believe she let you touch her."

He shrugged. It seemed silly to tell her he'd been courting her cat. Instead he said, "Why did you go out on the lake alone? You know how dangerous it could be at night."

It was her turn to shrug. "I figured you and your date would appreciate the privacy." There was no mockery in her tone, only a quiet resignation, and he shifted uncomfortably.

"You figured wrong. Tomorrow you're going to have to take me to town to pick up my car."

"Your car?" He'd startled her into looking at him and as her eyes met his, he felt an increase in the tension.

"She needed to get home and I didn't want to leave while you were out on the lake," he said. A flash of incredulity lit her gaze and she opened her mouth. Knowing that she was about to argue with him, he forestalled her by saying, "I need to talk to you." He didn't try to move closer; she was radiating distress signals that he knew he'd caused and at his words, she tensed as if she might flee and her gaze slid away from his.

"I—not now." She was looking at a spot somewhere around his shoulders rather than into his eyes, and he felt his frustration rise at the small gesture of avoidance.

"When, then?"

She moved to the door of her bedroom, making way for the cat who scampered in ahead of her. "We only have to be here for four more days and we'll have fulfilled the terms of the will. I'm sure we'll be called to the lawyer's office again when we return to Baltimore. You can say whatever needs to be said then."

She shut her bedroom door in his face almost before she'd uttered the last syllable, leaving him no opportunity to reply.

He stood perfectly still as he counted slowly to twenty. Even then, it took every ounce of self-persuasion he owned to make him turn and walk back to his own room. She'd never know how close he'd come to breaking down her door and demanding she listen to him.

She deliberately rose later than usual and took her time about getting down to the kitchen. As she'd hoped, he was already in his office. The last thing in the world she wanted to do was talk to him, so she grabbed a pastry and an orange and closeted herself in her workroom for the morning.

Images from the night before continued to flash through her brain until she felt like screaming. She didn't know what to feel, what to say, what to believe. He'd brought home a date, that much was unassailable. And even worse, he'd seen the warm welcome she had been prepared to offer him—until she realized he wasn't alone.

"Humiliated" didn't come close to describing how she'd felt. She'd bolted for the lake without even thinking about the inadvisability of paddling a canoe through the water in the dark.

But why had he pursued her? Was it really simply that he thought it wasn't safe to be out there alone at night? Giving the keys to his SUV to his date and letting her drive herself home seemed a little extreme, considering that he knew Ana was both a good boatsman and an excellent swimmer. She chose a pleasing shade of forest-green and began to form the felt on the wooden block, but when she realized she was still thinking about Garrett rather than the placement of the pert little brim she'd envisioned, she laid down the scissors and sighed through a mouthful of pins.

We have to talk. She could swear his eyes had been telegraphing an apology, but she wasn't sure what he would feel the need to apologize for. Unless it was to tell her he was sorry for asking someone else out, to tell her he only wanted her, Ana.

Fat chance of that happening in this lifetime. The animosity he'd shown early in their relationship might have faded, but she wasn't going to be stupid enough to let herself dream of happily-ever-after with him. What could—

"Ana?" Garrett's voice sounded as if it were just outside her studio door. "May I come in?"

"I—yes," she said, though her heart sank. "Come in." The last thing she wanted to do was conduct a postmortem on the events of last night. But he seemed determined. She might as well get it over with.

The door had been slightly ajar. He pushed it open and slowly came into the room, smiling tentatively at her. "I, uh, just wondered how your work is going. Are you getting as much accomplished as you'd hoped?"

She shrugged, trying for nonchalance when she met his eyes. "I didn't really have any quantifiable amount of work that I wanted to produce. But I've been working steadily every day, and I've got more designs in my head than I'll get finished in the next year, so I'd have to say it's going well."

"Good." He prowled the edges of the room. "What do you do with your finished pieces?"

"Pack them up and ship them to one of the two boutiques that've been selling me."

"No," he said with surprising patience. "What do you do with them here?"

"Oh." She waved a hand at the large closet along the wall. "They're in there."

Garrett walked to the closet. He had his hand on the doorknob when he stopped and looked over his shoulder at her. "May I?"

With the laser intensity of his blue eyes trained on her, she could barely think. "Sure," she managed.

He opened the closet doors wide so that the long rack she'd installed was completely visible, then stepped back a few paces and took it all in. He stepped closer, examining each set, picking up a hat here or a small clutch purse there.

Ana found she was holding her breath. She was attaching far too much importance to his opinion, she told herself sternly.

Then he turned to face her, shaking his head and smiling. "These are amazing. I bet women fight over them."

She stared at him. "You like my work?"

He grinned, and her heart skipped a beat at the flash of white teeth as his eyes warmed. "Don't sound so surprised."

She exhaled a shaky chuckle. "Artists are notoriously insecure about their efforts, no matter the medium. I'm no exception."

"When someone tells you they like something you look for the hidden criticism?"

"Something like that." She smiled back, glad for the easy banter.

Then he lifted his head and found her eyes again. "No wonder Robin thought you should be doing this full-time. These—" he indicated the completed pieces with a sweep of his hand "—are extraordinary."

"Thank you." She turned back to the pattern she'd been tracing.

"You know," he said, "you ought to be looking

for an investor. With enough capital, you could set yourself up to produce these things on a scale large enough to make it profitable."

She shook her head. "Right now it's just a labor of love. I don't want to share it with anyone else. I guess it's silly, but I feel very protective about my work."

He was silent as he looked again at one or two of the pieces on the rack. Then he swiveled back toward her. "Ana, if it's a question of money, I could—"

"No, thank you." She kept her voice calm. "I wouldn't be comfortable accepting money from you, even in the form of a loan."

He nodded. But in that instant, she saw something flicker in his eyes—and her heart contracted painfully. As if he'd said it aloud, she realized he was thinking that when he bought out her half of the cottage, she'd have more than enough money to start a small business. Despite what she'd told him, he still expected her to succumb to the lure of the eternal dollar.

And despite the physical pull between them, he clearly didn't trust her, or even like her very much.

At that moment, a sound that had been buzzing at the edges of her consciousness penetrated and she frowned. "Is that a car coming back here?"

"Maybe Eileen's bringing my truck back," Garrett said. He went to the big window that overlooked the lane and the grassy meadow beyond the birches. "Nope. It's an older-model black Jeep, I think."

"A black Jeep...?" She rose and walked to the window as the vehicle ground to a halt behind her old compact. The driver's door opened, and she recognized the occupant instantly. "Teddy!" Fear lent wings to her feet as she bolted down the stairs and through the house in record time. Her friend was still walking down the wide, shallow steps on the path when she met him.

"What happened?" she called as she neared him. "Is Nola all right? Do you need help—"

"Whoa!" Teddy was laughing. He grabbed her elbows and shook her lightly. "Everything's fine. In fact, everything's fantastic. We have identical twin daughters."

"Nola had the babies? Congratulations!" She was genuinely thrilled. She flung her arms around him and hugged him exuberantly. "When? Where are they? How can I help?"

Teddy was laughing as they drew apart. "Nola went into labor around nine-thirty and we went straight to the hospital. They were born at six forty-two and six forty-nine. They're a few weeks early but the doctor says they're in very good shape and as soon as they begin to gain a little weight we can bring them home."

"Six forty-two?" she cried. "They're only—" she checked her watch "—four hours old! Why are you out here?"

"Nola insisted," he told her. "We didn't want to tell you over the phone. She and the babies are sleeping right now so I was just twiddling my thumbs and drooling over their incubators." Then he fished in the pocket of his light jacket. "I brought pictures."

Ana squealed. She pored over the instant shots, exclaiming over the tiny, wrinkled faces in the pink knit caps. "They're beautiful! Do they have hair? What are you naming them?"

"They both have curly blond hair," he said, "though who knows if it will stay that way? And I think we're going to name them Jenna and Danielle."

"Jenna and Danielle," she repeated, still looking at the photos. "Oh, Teddy, thank you so much for coming all the way out here and bringing these." But when she tried to hand them back to him, he shook his head.

"These are yours to keep. Just promise you'll come in soon and meet them."

"I'll be there this afternoon," she promised him. They beamed at each other for a moment, then she took his face between her hands and kissed him noisily. "Congratulations again!"

He wrapped his arms around her in a bear hug and lifted her clear off the path for a moment. "Thanks."

"You'd better get back. One of your little girls might wake up and need her daddy." Ana turned him and tucked her elbow into his and they walked companionably back toward his Jeep.

He laughed. "I doubt that. Nola's breastfeeding so there's not a lot I can do for them right now."

"Except love them and cuddle them constantly." As he folded his lanky frame into the vehicle and the engine turned over, she waved energetically. "See you this afternoon!"

Seven

Garrett stood in the window where Ana had left him, frozen in place as he stared rigidly out the window. When Ana threw herself into the arms of the slender blond man, he made a guttural sound deep in his throat, a primitive growl of warning though there was no one to hear.

Was this the man she'd been sneaking off to meet? Teddy, she'd called him. He conveniently ignored the fact that she'd hardly been sneaking, that she'd even left him notes on several occasions telling him she'd taken a meal to friends in town. He watched as the guy gave her something—pictures, perhaps?—and they laughed and chatted together. When she took his face between her palms, kissing him as he reached out to enfold her in a hug, Garrett had seen enough.

Turning from the window, he stalked down the

stairs, intending to break up the little reunion. But as he came toward the cottage door, it opened and Ana strolled in. She was beaming. "Guess what?"

"Is that who you've been taking all the meals to for the past couple of weeks?" he demanded. "You told me you didn't know anyone up here, but the first damned time I turn around, you're cooking for some guy every couple of days."

All the happy light drained from her expression. She stopped just inside the door, staring at him as if he were crazy. Maybe he was. If so, it was her fault. But a little voice inside him cautioned: *Just because you want her doesn't mean you own her.*

In a tone cool enough to lower the room temperature by ten degrees, she said, "Yes. That's who I've been taking meals to. I met him the first time I went to town." Then her eyes changed and he could see the growing fury behind the searing glance she shot his way. "How dare you?"

"I—"

"How dare you?" she repeated. "You've been jumping to conclusions—*wrong* conclusions—since the first day we met. You think I met some guy and promptly jumped into bed with him, don't you?"

"Not exactly." He knew he'd overstepped the boundaries they'd drawn in recent days. Hell, he'd overstepped the bounds of common courtesy a long time ago. What was it about her that brought out the caveman in him?

"Ha." She stepped toward him and raised a hand and he instinctively caught her wrist.

"Wait a minute. Just wait a minute."

"I will not." It was a snarl. She shook her hair back from where it had worked its way free of the loose braid she'd worn while she worked. "Let go of me. I want to show you something."

He glanced at the hand he still held then, and realized that she had photographs clutched between her fingers. Feeling a little foolish, he released her. "Look, I'm sorry—"

"At least you got that part right," she hurled at him. She raised the photographs and shoved them beneath his nose, practically vibrating with anger. Her hand was shaking so badly he couldn't see the images so he plucked them from her fingers and looked at…babies?

"Those," she said pointedly, "are my friends Teddy and Nola's twin baby girls who were just born this morning. Nola's had a difficult pregnancy and appreciated the meals and the help I offered. They're both lovely people and I've enjoyed making friends in the area." She stopped. "Why am I explaining myself to you?" she demanded. She snatched the photos from him and turned toward the steps.

He grabbed her arm and spun her around. "Wait."

"No!" She wrenched away and stormed toward the stairs. "I am sick and tired of being judged by you. I cannot *wait* for the next four days to be over so that I never have to set eyes on you again."

Garrett stood in the middle of the living room as she vanished up the steps. Her door slammed with a resounding thud and he winced. He'd never seen her in a real temper before but he should have guessed that with that hair there was the potential for fireworks.

He heaved a sigh and rubbed the back of his neck. Dammit. She was right. He had been judging her, jumping to conclusions again, and he felt like a fool. Slowly he mounted the steps. Ana's door was shut and Roadkill sat just outside it, a tentative paw raised and planted against the wood.

"What's the matter, girl?" he asked. "Did she lock you out?" Stepping forward, he knocked on the door. "Ana?"

"Go away."

Oh, hell. Her voice sounded thick and he knew she was crying. And it was his fault. Again. "Your cat wants in," he told the door.

There was a soft scuffling sound and the door swung open just wide enough for the cat to enter. But as it closed again, Garrett stuck out his foot and held it open. There was a pause as she realized what he was doing, then the pressure on the door eased and he pushed it open.

Ana stood in the center of the room, her back to him.

"I was jealous." The bald admission hung in the air between them.

He saw her slowly shake her head, as if the words made no sense. "What?"

Crossing to stand directly behind her, he repeated the words with more conviction. "I was jealous."

She turned to face him, eyes wide and shocked. "But...but why?"

He cleared his throat, raising one hand to cradle

her cheek, sweeping his thumb along the smooth skin of her throat and jaw as he wiped away her tears. "Can you honestly tell me you don't feel it? There's something between us, Ana, something that gets stronger every minute we're together. I know it's wrong to want you," he said hoarsely, "but I'm tired of fighting myself." Beneath his cupped hand, the bones of her jaw felt fragile, the skin silky smooth. He stroked the pad of his thumb across her lips.

"It's not wrong," she said against his thumb. "I've been wanting to explain for the longest time—"

"No. No explanations." He was seized by a sudden, irrational fear. He could sense the intimacy in the moment; words would destroy it. With slow deliberation, he bent his head and replaced his thumb with his lips. "Just this," he said. He slid his arms around her and pulled her to him, growling with deep satisfaction as his hungry body was cushioned by her soft, yielding female form.

For a moment, she stood docilely in his embrace, neither rejecting nor accepting his caresses. But as he slanted his lips more fully over hers and teased the tender bowed line of her upper lip with his tongue, her carefully neutral posture softened and she melted against him as she made a small sound. Her mouth opened to admit him to the hot, sweet depths, and her arms came up, first to rest tentatively on his shoulders, and then to twine more securely around his neck as the kiss deepened and the undeniable sparks between them caught and blazed high.

He'd felt himself getting hard the moment she'd turned to face him in the intimate confines of her bedroom. As she stood on tiptoe and pressed herself to him, he slid one hand down the elegant line of her back and palmed one of the sweet, rounded globes of her bottom, hauling her higher against him, pushing his eager flesh more firmly into the heated notch of her thighs. The fit was so satisfying that he groaned aloud.

Then Ana raised one leg and hooked it high around his hip, opening herself to him completely and suddenly he knew there was only one way for this embrace to end. Though he hadn't woken up planning it, he was going to make love to Ana Birch today.

Pivoting, he took the few strides to the side of the bed with her still clinging to him. He set her on her feet on the braided rug beside it, then used his tongue to dip and circle, to slip into and explore every hidden corner of her mouth as he pulled handfuls of T-shirt free of her shorts.

He'd wanted her for so long. He'd fantasized about her silky body, the full curves of her breasts, the gold-brushed curls between her legs…and she was going to be his. Finding the hem of her shirt, he drew it up and off, then resumed kissing her while she fumbled with his shirt. When she had it off, he drew her close again, unhooking her bra and dragging it away, then pressing her satiny flesh to his. The feel of her bared breasts against his naked torso was a staggering delight, but he drew her away so that he could look down at the beauty he'd uncovered. Her skin was a creamy ivory, the pale rosy shade of her nipples a stunning contrast, and he brought both hands up to cup the sweet weighted mounds in his palms, brushing his thumbs over her nipples until her eyes went blind with pleasure and she clutched his shoulders, pleading, "Please..."

"Please what?"

Her hands slipped to the fastening of his shorts, wordlessly indicating her needs. But when she got there, instead of dealing with the button, her small fingers slipped lower to press and explore him through his pants. He nearly leaped out of his skin at the hesitant, intimate touch and he couldn't prevent the shudder of desire that danced down his spine as he rolled his hips heavily into her hand. Reluctantly leaving her breasts, he dealt with his shorts, shoving them and his briefs down and off in the same motion. In another moment he had hers off as well.

Then he urged her backward onto the bed, coming down beside her. He bent over her and claimed her mouth again, giving all his attention to her sweet, responsive mouth until they were both breathing in ragged gulps. When he finally lifted his head, she buried her face in his throat. He explored her body with his free hand, stroking and petting every inch of her yielding feminine treasures until finally he swept his fingers down to tangle in the silky thatch of curls at the vee of her legs.

Ana gasped beneath his mouth when he extended one long finger, slipping it slowly, inexorably down through the damp folds of skin to the slick warmth inside. He pressed and circled her there, dragging his mouth down her body to suckle strongly at her breast as her back arched off the bed and she held his head to her with trembling fingers. Her hips were rising and falling in rhythm with his finger, steadily caressing his hot, hard length where he pressed against her thigh. At one such rise he slipped the single digit deeply into her body, pressing upward. She uttered one short, sharp scream and her body convulsed in his arms.

His own body was screaming for attention as he drank in her response. As she shook and trembled beneath him, he quickly withdrew his finger and rose over her, kneeing her thighs apart and guiding himself to her. She was hot, very wet, and though he knew he should go slowly, at the first yielding of her tender flesh, his hips flexed and thrust forward in one great spasm that propelled him deep inside her as she still quivered in the grip of her own ecstasy.

She screamed again and arched up against him, her hands sliding to his buttocks and pulling him sharply to her, deeper and deeper as her inner muscles flexed and squeezed. He was caught in the grip of an irresistible force, snared in a hot, silky net of need. He could feel himself losing control, abandoning all attempts to hold back and make it last, and in the next moment, he was seized by his own finish, hips thudding against her, back arched, neck straining as he delivered his seed deep inside her.

Inside her! Instantly he tried to pull out but her hands still held him to her and his own body resisted his commands. Unable to resist, he gave himself to the shivering, delicious sensations and let his body take over.

When the last spasm had ended and they both lay

limp and drained, Garrett raised his head from the pillow where his face was buried.

"Are you on the pill?"

Ana froze. The shock in her face told him before she even opened her mouth. "No." She closed her eyes. "I'm so sorry. I wasn't thinking."

He propped himself on his elbows and kissed each of her eyelids. "I'm the one who should have been thinking." He grinned crookedly. "But I was busy." Then he sobered. "Don't worry. We'll deal with it if there's a consequence."

Her eyes opened and she stared solemnly up at him. "I can't believe you don't keep anything with you."

He shrugged one shoulder. "I think I hoped that if I didn't have any protection I'd have the sense not to give in to…this."

She stiffened, and he realized immediately how he had sounded. "Ana," he said. She wouldn't look at him. "Ana." He dropped his head and kissed her until she responded, then lifted his head and looked deep into her eyes. "I didn't mean I don't find you desirable. I was trying to…I don't know, keep to the high road, I guess. Right now I can't remember why that seemed so important."

She relaxed again and he bent to capture her lips once more until he realized she was shifting uncomfortably. He needed to move; she was far too small to support his weight. Withdrawing and sliding to one side, he pulled her into his arms. Tucking her head beneath his chin, he lay silently, watching the patterns of dancing leaves in the sunlight on the far wall. If he'd ever felt so content before, he couldn't recall it.

Ana's warm body snuggled bonelessly against him, the wild curls of her hair drifted over his shoulder and turned to fire in a ray of light that lay across their bodies. He felt…protective, he decided, cuddling her closer. And possessive. She was his now.

"Garrett?" Ana ran a lethargic hand through the dense mat of silky dark hair across his breastbone, following its path as it arrowed into a thin line down past his navel, then bloomed again beneath.

"Hmm?"

"What did you mean, we'd deal with it if I were to get pregnant?"

He went still beside her, alert to an odd tone in her musical voice. "I don't know," he said. "I just wanted you to know I wouldn't walk away and leave you to handle something like that alone."

"Because I would never—I couldn't—"

"I would want a child if it were to happen." He turned his head and kissed her temple, soothing her agitation as he realized what was troubling her. "Is it likely?"

She thought for a moment. "Likely? I suppose it's possible." She sighed. "I always promised myself that a child of mine wouldn't grow up without its father like I did."

It was his turn to still. "Why would it?" he asked carefully. "Unlike the guy that fathered you, I'm not married to someone else and I'm not about to run from my responsibilities." A child…with Ana. A vague shiver of anticipation tightened the muscles of his stomach. He could think of worse fates. In fact, he wasn't sure he could think of anything he'd like better.

Then he realized that Ana hadn't answered him.

Tightening his arm, he drew her up onto his chest and put his other arm about her as well. "Let's not get ourselves bent out of shape for no reason, all right?"

The curtain of her hair shut out the sunlight as she looked down at him and her eyes were dark and mysterious. "All right," she finally said.

He ran one hand up the silky expanse of her back and threaded his fingers through her hair, cradling her skull and pulling her head down until their lips met. Though he'd intended it as a kiss of comfort, her instant, wholehearted response brought his body leaping alive again, and he finally had to set her from him with a grimace. "No more sex until I have a chance to get to a store."

He felt her body move in silent laughter. "Not…anything?"

"You little tease." He rolled, pinning her beneath him. "I'm not taking any more chances on forgetting. Come on. Let's go to the store." As he tugged her out of bed behind him, he acknowledged that condoms were a necessity. Now. Making love to Ana was addictive; already he wanted her again. But he didn't simply want to play games, as she'd intimated. No. When he made love to her, something within him demanded the basic, primitive need to be buried deep inside her.

But as he tossed her clothes at her, she shook her head. "I need a shower."

He grinned. "Why? We're just going right back to bed as soon as we get home."

"But I promised to visit Nola and the twins, remember?" She brushed past him, lithe and lovely in her nakedness, but he put out a hand and caught her wrist. Turning her to him, he took a long survey, drinking in all the fine details he'd missed in the frantic rush to completion earlier. Her hips were slender; her legs long. He already knew that, as he'd known her breasts were full and her arms lightly muscled. What he hadn't known, however, was the lovely pale rose of the crests of her breasts, the glint of gold in the thatch of hair between her legs, the way her torso nipped in to her waist and flared so gently out to her hips again.

Ana was staring at him. "What?"

He smiled at her. "You're beautiful."

Her face softened. Then, to his dismay, her eyes filled with tears. "Thank you." She tugged her hand free. "I'll make it fast in the shower."

The trip to town was quiet, though not awkward. Garrett didn't talk much on the way but when she'd climbed into the passenger seat he threaded his fingers through hers and leaned across the console to give her a lingering kiss. Ana didn't talk, either, half-afraid to damage the new, fragile relationship they shared.

She had to tell him about her father. Today. She'd tried earlier, honestly tried, but he'd cut her off and once he'd begun to kiss her she'd forgotten all about it. But she knew she needed to get it out into the open. This evening, she would tell him.

Thinking about her father led to thoughts of her mother. A wave of nostalgia swept over her. What would her mother think of Garrett? She slid a sideways glance across the seat toward him.

He was watching her.

Flustered, she looked away again, and he gave a low chuckle. "What are you thinking?"

"Not the same thing you're thinking," she said tartly, and he laughed again. "If you really want to know, I was wondering what my mother would have thought of you."

"She would have thought I was handsome and charming," he said promptly.

It was her turn to laugh. "And modest."

There was a small, comfortable silence between them. Then he said, "Tell me about her."

She was warmed by the interest in his voice. "She was a painter. A very, very good one. Her name is well-known in international art circles." Her voice caught and Garrett squeezed her fingers. When the lump in her throat had eased, she said, "Tell me how your mother met Robin."

She saw the smile that lifted the corner of his mouth. "It was a setup."

"A setup?"

He flashed her a grin. "My mother was a bit on the helpless side. Her skills were limited to being a good hostess and keeping a perfect house. After my father died she was completely over her head. Her friends started introducing her to their friends, hoping that a man would come along to take care of her again."

"Did she love Robin?"

"She adored him." His voice grew reflective. "I think she was far more in love with him than he ever was with her."

"What makes you say that?" Every small snippet of information she could add to her meager store of details about her father were precious, even those regarding his life with the family of which she hadn't been a part.

Garrett shrugged. "For a long time, it was just a sense that I had. He was always wonderful to Mother, but there was something...something a little sad in his eyes sometimes."

He raised her hand to his lips and kissed her fingers. "He was such a great guy. Getting him for a stepfather was the best thing that could have happened to me."

She was sure that was true and she stroked the back of his hand with her thumb as his voice thickened.

"I still can't believe he's gone," he confessed. "At least once a day I reach for the phone to call him before I remember that he won't be there."

Her own throat was too tight to speak. All she could do was stroke his hand in wordless sympathy.

They didn't talk again after that until they reached town, and she was content to sit beside him with his hand enclosing hers. It felt *right* with him, and she supposed that Robin's plan to throw them together had worked in that regard. Living in the same small space had accustomed them to each other's quirks and routines and given them a level of comfort they'd never have known under other circumstances.

At home again after picking up his truck and stopping by the hospital, Garrett hurried her through the door, then tossed their purchases on the kitchen counter and turned to take her in his arms. She snuggled against him, loving the solid feel of his big body, the warmth of his arms around her, the perfect fit of her head in the crook of his neck.

"Want to go for a canoe ride?" he said against her ear.

She shivered as his lips found the delicate shell and he bit down gently on her earlobe. "Th-that would be nice."

"Yeah." But he made no move to release her. Against her belly, she could feel the rising length of his desire and her breath grew short as her body softened and tingled. She slowly rubbed herself back and forth over him the slightest bit, brushing her sensitive nipples across the hard planes of his chest.

Garrett lifted a hand and circled her throat, tipping her chin up with his thumb. He bent, covering her mouth with his in a long, languid kiss as his hand slipped down to shape and stroke her breast, tugging at the tender peak until she was writhing in his arms.

"I think," he murmured against her mouth, "that the lake will have to wait."

She fumbled blindly along the edge of the counter with one hand until she found the bag from the store. Withdrawing the box of protection he'd purchased, she held it as he lifted her into his arms and carried her up the stairs and into her room, where he lay her on the bed. It took him only moments to methodically strip away her garments and then his.

She opened her arms to welcome him, sighing with relief when his full weight came down atop her. "Oh, Garrett," she whispered, "I lo—" Then she stopped, shocked by the words that had nearly escaped. *I love you.*

"Hmm?" He was kissing a path down her neck and across her collarbone and she shivered as his beard-roughened skin dragged over her.

"I like the way you do that," she mumbled, but her brain was still reeling at the near-slip. Although she wasn't sure, she suspected that Garrett still wasn't ready to admit to anything deeper than a physical attraction. But once he knew about her father…then, she hoped, he would be able to see that what they shared could be permanent.

The next three days were idyllic, if he didn't think about the fact that they were about to end. On the afternoon before they were to leave, they'd spent the day packing up everything nonessential and putting dustcovers over the furniture in preparation for the long winter when the cottage would stand alone in the snow.

But after they'd cleaned and put away the deck furniture, Garrett reached out and tossed her up over his shoulder as he headed inside.

"Garrett!" Laughing, Ana pounded her small fists on his back. "What are you doing?"

"Taking my woman to bed."

"Your woman? Feeling a little primitive today, are we?" She gasped as he let her bounce onto the mattress, then followed her down before she could wriggle away.

"Feeling a little primitive *every* day," he corrected, fastening his teeth lightly on her earlobe and flicking his tongue along the tender rim. "You belong to me and I intend to make sure you don't forget it." Then, as if he'd realized just how he sounded, he dropped his head and kissed her, a slow, lingering mating of lips and tongues that roused her sluggish pulse even as his words roused the love hidden in her heart. She wrapped her arms around his muscled shoulders and pressed herself to him, offering her love in the only way she would allow herself, and within moments, they were naked and rolling together across the wide bed.

More than an hour later, a rumble of thunder disturbed their lethargic contentment.

Garrett turned his head and looked toward the window that faced out over the lake. "Looks like we're in for a storm."

"Mmm-hmm." Ana pressed an openmouthed kiss to his bare chest. "The weather service called for thunderstorms all along the coast this evening."

He sighed. "I'd better go down and bring the canoe onto the beach. If the lake gets rough, it's too fragile to be slammed against the dock."

She made a small moue of discontent but obediently sat up and reached for the closest garment at hand, which happened to be his T-shirt. "I'll close all the windows and stack the deck chairs."

Together they walked down the stairs. Ana went out onto the deck while he moved on through the kitchen. A moment later, he appeared again, heading down the path toward the dock. As he walked, he turned and called to her, "The back door was open. I must not have closed it firmly when we came in."

She couldn't prevent the smug smile that spread across her face as she surveyed him. All he wore were his pants and the muscles in his chest and arms rippled as he gestured. "Guess you had other things on your mind."

He grinned in return. "Guess I did." Then his grin faded. "You'd better check on the cat. I doubt she got out, but just in case..."

Roadkill. She felt her own good mood flee. The cat needed medication twice a day to ward off the seizures she suffered. Without it, her brain would succumb to the frightening fits more and more frequently. Roadkill would probably die if she were left on her own now.

She checked every room, every corner, every nook and cranny where she thought the cat might be likely to hide. She liked small spaces, and had been known to squeeze under low chairs and into the picnic basket in the pantry. But she wasn't anywhere.

Garrett came in the door just as she was out of ideas, and she turned to him fearfully. "I can't find her anywhere. I think she might have gotten out."

"Are you sure she isn't here?" He moved past her to the counter and took out a couple of tins of cat food. "Let's open this and wave it around. If she hears the top pop or smells it, she'll come running."

Ana nodded, reassured by his calm confidence.

"Okay." She took a deep, steadying breath. "If she comes, she's getting both cans at once."

He smiled, placing one large hand on her shoulder and massaging briefly. "You take the upstairs. I'll check down here."

She moved quickly to obey, but after a few minutes of futile calling and letting the noxious odor of canned cat food waft through the house, she slowly came down the stairs, feeling tears rising despite her best efforts. "She isn't here, is she?" she asked, biting down hard on her lip to keep it from quavering.

He hesitated for a moment, then shook his head. "It doesn't look like it. She must have sneaked out that door." He set down the cat food on the counter in the kitchen. "I'm sorry. I should have made sure that door was closed."

"It wasn't your fault." She tried to smile. "Neither one of us was thinking about the door."

His expression softened. "No," he said. "We weren't."

The sudden sound of rain hissing against the windows interrupted him as the storm unleashed a deluge that pounded down on the cottage and the pines and birches surrounding it. Lightning flashed and thunder clapped almost simultaneously, making her jump. Garrett gathered her close.

"Look," he said. "If she is out there, she's probably scared silly and will be thrilled to see you. Get your keys. You can drive down the lane in the car and call her from the window."

"What will you be doing?" She was already moving toward the hook that held the car keys.

"I'll check around the outside of the cabin." As she shrugged into a rain slicker and prepared to make the dash to her car, he took her by the elbow and held her back for a moment. "Promise me," he said intensely, "that you won't get out of the car. These storms can be dangerous."

"You're going out in it," she said.

"One of us has to. There's no sense in both of us taking unnecessary chances."

She hesitated. "I'm afraid I'll see her and she won't come."

He shoved one of the open cans of cat food into her free hand. "She'll come. Stay in the car."

Reluctantly she nodded. "All right." Then she went into his arms and kissed him quickly. "Please be careful."

Eight

Garrett waited until the driving rain obscured her taillights as Ana drove out the lane. Then he took the other can of food, grabbed a flashlight and stepped out onto the porch, taking a deep breath. The rain was still drumming down with stinging force. There was another flash of lightning, but this time the thunder was delayed by several seconds, indicating that the storm was no longer directly overhead.

Where would the cat have gone? He looked around. It hadn't been raining when she'd gone out, so she might have moved some distance away from the cottage, but he'd bet she'd found cover once the full force of the storm hit.

He plunged off the porch into the pouring rain. First he circled the cabin, calling the cat as he checked all the spaces around the foundation and under the

porches where a small animal might hide. As he knelt
to shine the light into the recesses of the lean-to where
he stored split logs, he hoped that skunks didn't like
cat food. Unfortunately—or fortunately, he thought
wryly—nothing of any species appeared to be hiding
there.

As he approached the cove, he crunched over the
gravel, heading for the far end of the beach. But as
he drew abreast of the canoe he'd overturned above
the waterline only minutes before the storm started,
he thought he heard a sound. A cat sound.

He stopped in his tracks. Pivoting, he shone the
beam of the flashlight beneath the canoe. It reflected
eerie light from a pair of close-set eyes. Cat eyes.

Garrett closed his own eyes in relief. "Roadkill?
Come here, you ungrateful cat."

A plaintive meow answered him clearly through
the diminishing patter of the rain, but the eyes didn't
move.

He sighed. Kneeling, he shoved the tin of cat food
right to the edge of the canoe. "Come here, you mo-
ronic critter," he said in what he hoped was a loving
tone. "You're worrying your pretty mistress to
death."

Roadkill meowed again, and then the eyes moved.
He moved just as fast, pulling the food out of reach,
out into the open. His other hand hovered just above
the opening where the cat would have to emerge.

And he waited.

The eyes blinked, then moved again, slowly. Inch
by incremental inch, the small tiger cat came slinking
out from beneath the canoe on her belly. She looked

completely spooked, her eyes wild and dark, and he could see it wouldn't take much to send her running into the unfamiliar terrain again. He kept a firm hand on the can, unmoving, and eventually she decided she wanted the food more than she feared his presence. As she settled down to her feast, he put a large, firm hand on the back of her neck and took a fistful of cat scruff.

Roadkill froze. Quickly he pulled her up against his chest and shoved the cat food beneath her nose as she began to struggle. "Here—ouch! Dammit, cat— eat!"

Apparently realizing that her days of freedom were at an end, she relaxed in his arms and buried her face in the can of food he offered.

He looked down. Two furrows of cat scratches oozed blood just below his left collarbone. "I should have let you go," he grumbled to the little animal as he climbed the path. "You're a—"

"You found her!" Ana was coming down the wide steps above the house. "Oh, Garrett, where was she? I can't believe she came to you!"

"She didn't exactly come to *me*," he said ruefully as she reached them and lifted the cat from his arms. "She was a lot more excited about the food."

Ana preceded him into the house, cooing and cuddling the little ingrate, who streaked out of the room and up the steps to the second floor the moment Ana set her down. They both laughed, and Ana turned to him with a shining face and launched herself into his arms. "Thank you, thank you, thank you!"

He still held the cat food and the flashlight, but she

wound her arms around his neck and pressed herself against him, fervently raining kisses across his chest and up his chin. Unable to resist the invitation, he reached behind her to set down the items, then put both hands on her bottom and hauled her up against him as she found his mouth and began to kiss him.

She was a wild thing in his embrace, burning him alive with her mouth and her tongue as he let her take the lead. Slowly she slipped down his body, pausing a moment when her mouth brushed over the cat scratches. "We should clean those," she purred. "They can be nasty." But she already was moving on, finding his flat male nipple with her swirling tongue, nipping at him until the sweet sensation plucked a strong answering chord in his groin and he threaded his fingers through her hair and pressed her to him.

"Later," he said hoarsely. "We'll clean them later."

Ana slid farther down his body, her mouth following the line of hair that arrowed down his torso, her tongue probing his navel as her hands worked at the soaking fabric of his trousers.

He closed his eyes and leaned back against the wall, groaning as he felt the fabric give way. Cool air washed over his erect flesh, then Ana's warm hand closed around him, easing him free of the clinging material. "Lord," he said in a guttural tone that he barely recognized as his own, "Ana, stop. No, don't stop." He bared his teeth in a feral smile as she sat back on her heels and looked up the length of his body with triumphant eyes.

Her hand moved slowly over him as she returned the smile with a slow, confident feminine expression that tightened his body in another wild rush of sensation. He saw her intent in her eyes moments before she leaned forward, bathing him with her sweet breath for an instant before her mouth closed over him.

His breath wheezed out in an agonizing sound of pleasure too great to be borne and his hands clenched in her hair as her questing fingers brushed between his legs and clasped his thighs. She loved him with hot, wild strokes of mouth and hand, using her tongue to bring him quickly to the point of no return. As he gave himself to her sweet ministrations, the storm broke over his head, driving him to a harsh, breathtaking climax that left his knees shaking as he stared blindly at the ceiling, gasping for breath.

Ana rose fluidly to her feet and took his hand while he was still trying to regulate his breathing, saying softly, "Let's go upstairs."

But as she turned away, he used the handclasp to drag her back against him. To his shock, he realized that all she wore was the T-shirt she'd pulled on earlier. He yanked up the fabric in handfuls and pressed her smooth bare curves hard against him, seeking her mouth as her warm female form ignited a desire he'd have sworn he couldn't possibly feel again so quickly.

"Ana," he muttered against her mouth as his hands streaked over her body possessively. "Do you know what you do to me?" Cradling her skull, he held her head against his shoulder as he kissed her long and deeply, loving her mouth as thoroughly as she'd loved him minutes before.

When he lifted his head, she raised a hand to his lean jaw, and her eyes were dazed with soft pleasure. "Garrett," she murmured. "I love you."

The husky words confirmed something he had barely allowed himself to consider, and he was shocked by the fierce masculine satisfaction rushing through him. Although he couldn't pinpoint the moment when his life had changed, he knew it had. Forever. He could no longer imagine his future without Ana in it, could no longer imagine his life without her.

But at the same time, a desperate voice in his head shouted for caution. Very deliberately, he shut off the thoughts clamoring for his attention. He could think later. Right now...right now it was enough simply to feel.

Ana stirred in his arms and he realized her words still hung between them. Touching his mouth lightly to her forehead, he said, "Let's go upstairs." He set his mouth on her again and lifted her into his arms at the same time. Her arms went around his neck as he carried her through the living room and up the stairs to the bed they'd shared through the hours of the morning.

I love you.

The scary thing, Garrett decided as he lay sleepless several hours later, was that he'd wanted to say the words back to her...*had* nearly blurted out those three small, single-syllable words that could irrevocably change a person's life. His life.

And though everything in him had urged him to

throw caution to the winds, he'd held his tongue. He cared for her, cared for her in a way that he had to acknowledge he'd never felt before about any woman. Even Kammy. Especially Kammy. He'd thought she was special, had thought he'd loved her. But now…now he knew better. And the knowledge made it even more difficult not to respond to Ana's declaration.

But he couldn't. Wouldn't, because he knew these feelings weren't real. Thank God his last attempt at intimacy had ended as it had; he was a lot smarter because of it. Though he'd hated Kammy at the time, now he realized he was lucky to have learned the truth about her before the wedding.

So what was the truth about Ana? He desperately wanted to believe she wanted to spend the rest of her life with him, as well. But he couldn't believe it was that easy. The facts gave him pause.

He had money. Ana needed money. Even if he did buy out her half of the cabin, it wouldn't be a sum that would last her any length of time. Realistically it would barely be enough to allow her to properly set up the kind of small business she had in mind.

The logical extension of their new involvement would be for her to move in with him. Was that what she'd been angling for all along?

Ana mumbled something and shifted in his arms, and he realized his embrace had tightened around her. Carefully he relaxed the tense muscles of his shoulders. She snuggled more closely against him again and a pleasant sexual shiver ran down his spine as her warm breath feathered across his throat. Her body was soft and pliant, her sleep deep and peaceful. He liked the way she felt in his arms, the way she fit so perfectly against his body, the way she moaned and arched up to him when he took her. He probably could spend the rest of his life in bed with her and never mind it for a minute.

No, she didn't really love him, he decided, though she even might believe she did. A few weeks ago, he'd have thought she was using those words as Kammy had, in order to wrap him around her finger for money or security or whatever her particular needs happened to be. Now he knew that wasn't the case, at least, not the *whole* case. If Ana said she loved him, she thought she was telling the truth.

I love you. It was the sex talking. It had to be. And that, of course, was why he'd nearly responded. It was easy to confuse the two. Great sex produced strong emotion, and a lot of people believed that was the same as love.

He knew better, he reminded himself again, though perhaps *she* didn't realize there was a difference. Ultimately it didn't matter. If she wanted to fool herself, it was fine by him. The bottom line was that he'd sworn never to let himself be manipulated by a woman who might be after his money ever again. Ana wasn't like his former fiancée in most ways, true, but…there was a niggling corner of dark doubt in his mind. She needed money. He had money. He was merely being realistic. The bottom line…if he'd been penniless, would Ana still tell him she loved him?

He didn't know. He honestly didn't. But as long as he accepted the real bottom line, there was no reason

he couldn't enjoy her for as long as they were together.

And they were going to be together for a while, of
that he was positive. Whatever her relationship with
Robin had been, he no longer cared. She'd made his
stepfather's last years of life happy, had given him
joy and pleasure that he clearly hadn't known before.
How could he resent that?

She woke when Garrett eased his arm from beneath
her neck and slid from the warm nest of the bed.
Slitting her eyes against the early-morning sunlight
that flowed in the large window, she watched as he
padded naked across the floor to the bathroom. God,
he was beautiful. His legs were long and straight, and
the lean hollows of his buttocks made her palms tin-
gle with the need to trace the smooth skin. His shoulders, in contrast to his narrow waist and hips, looked
as wide as a house.

As he disappeared into the bathroom, she inched
over into the warm depression he'd left. She didn't
want to wake up, didn't want the day to begin.

Things would be different between them now, she
feared. He hadn't responded to her declaration of love
last night. She hadn't really expected him to, hadn't
really even intended to say the words herself, but
they'd burst out without warning. She wasn't
sorry…exactly. But she was a little nervous. Would
it change things between them? Would he step back
from the warmth and intimacy they shared? Yesterday, she'd assumed that when they returned to Bal-

timore they'd be returning together, making plans together.

His silence last night had erased all her assumptions.

He came back out of the bathroom without warning, and before she could close her eyes and play
possum, his startlingly blue, stunningly beautiful eyes
had snared her gaze. His held a warm intimacy.
"Good morning," he said as he crossed to the bed.

"Good morning." She cleared her throat. He
perched on the edge of the bed, cupping the ball of
her shoulder where it was uncovered by the sheets.
His thumb gently stroked her sensitive skin.

"Want to go for a swim, sweetheart?" he asked.

"That would be great." Her heart lurched at the
endearment even as she told herself it meant nothing.
Then she screeched as he tossed back the blanket and
scooped her into his arms. She clung to his neck as
he strode down the stairs, balancing her on his knee
while he unlocked the door. Then he carried her out
of the cottage and down the path to the lake.

"Garrett! Put me down! We can't just run around
naked."

He paused and looked down at her, laughing.
"Why not? You've done it before." Negotiating the
steps to the dock, he walked all the way to the end.
And before she realized what he intended, he shifted
sideways, lifted her higher and swung her out over
the water, releasing her at the last second and she
splashed into the cold water with a shocked excla-
mation.

When she surfaced, pushing handfuls of wet corkscrew curls back from her face, he was treading water beside her, still chuckling. She couldn't hide the bubble of amusement that rose as she turned over onto her back and floated beside him. "Very funny. You know what they say about paybacks."

He gave a mock-shiver. "I'm shaking in my shoes." Then he reached out and pulled her to him, moving around the side of the dock into water where he could touch bottom, though Ana still couldn't. The water made their bodies slippery and silky and as his thigh slid between hers and his mouth descended, she forgot to laugh. Against her lips, he whispered, "There's something I've always wanted to try in the water. Want to share a first with me?"

He was hard against her belly as she wrapped her legs around his hips and offered herself to him. "I'd love to."

"There's something I've been wanting to talk to you about," she said an hour later, industriously buttering two slices of toast.

"I know." He was busy flipping over the eggs.

"You do?"

"Yeah," he said. "Today's the day. As of today we are officially the owners of Eden Cottage. And my original offer still stands. I'll be happy to pay you full market value for your half."

She was stunned. "That wasn't…it's not…" She'd supposed they had gotten beyond that. It was a shock to realize that the time they'd spent here together had done nothing to alter Garrett's thinking. "I still don't want to sell it," she said carefully.

There was a moment of silence. She could sense the tension growing between them. "You need the money," he said, "don't you? I thought you wanted to get your business off the ground."

"I do." She could barely speak around the lump in her throat that threatened to choke her. "But this place has become very special to me. Robin wanted me to have it. To share it with you."

He didn't say anything.

And suddenly she realized that this was the moment, though she hadn't planned it as carefully as she'd intended. The time she'd been avoiding for weeks. She took a deep breath. "The reason it's so special," she said, "is that Robin was very special to me. He was my father."

Garrett went still. "Ana—"

"Robin was my father." She rushed on when he only stared at her in silence, his gaze dark and unfathomable. "He and my mother fell in love but he wouldn't leave his first wife because she was already mentally ill. When my mother found out she was pregnant, she decided to go away."

Garrett's eyes narrowed and he spoke for the first time. "Why? Seems like that would have given her more leverage to press for marriage."

His words hurtled against her like hailstones and she felt a defensive retort rise. "You didn't know my mother," she said in clipped tones, lifting her chin. "She wouldn't have wanted to put Robin in the position of having to make a choice that would have haunted him forever. And at that point in time, no one had any idea how long Maggie would live."

"And you know this because…?" There was little inflection in his cool tone.

"When my mother realized she was terminally ill, she wrote Robin and me each a letter to be delivered by her attorney…afterward." She had to stop and swallow the grief that rose. "When Robin learned that he had a daughter, he was on my doorstep the very next day. My letter, as you can imagine, was quite a shock, since I thought my father had died years ago."

"I'm sure it was," Garrett murmured.

Encouraged, she said, "Mrs. Davenport told me that Robin and my mother built this place together. They only spent one summer here together before she left."

Garrett dropped his face into his hands and pressed hard against his forehead. "Ana…" He hesitated.

She looked at him expectantly. Surely now he understood why she didn't want to sell. And he also must realize that his assumptions about her had been completely off-base from the very beginning. "No apologies are necessary," she said. "I intended to tell you long ago, but you made me so mad I decided to let you think whatever you wanted. And then I meant to, several times, but it just was never right, and then last night—"

"Ana." His voice was firmer, and she stopped in midsentence. "You don't have to do this," he said quietly. "If you want to keep half the cottage that badly, you can have it." He patted his knee. "Come here."

Confused, she allowed him to take her hand and

pull her down. What did he mean, she didn't have to do this? Do what?

"I want you," he said, looking deep into her eyes. "Your past isn't important to me. I'd like you to come to live with me."

At first the words made no sense. But then her paralyzed brain began to sort out sounds and meanings again and she nearly cried aloud as the ugly truth pierced her heart. He didn't believe her! Dear heaven, in all the ways she'd envisioned this scene playing out, that he wouldn't believe her hadn't even been on her mental movie screen.

"Ana?" His beautiful eyes were studying her, waiting for her answer.

She was dying inside, her heart shriveling into a dried-up, unusable state, and the cold calm of utter shock took over. *You can't break down,* she told herself. *Not in front of Garrett.* "For how long?" It was the only response that came into her head, not a question to which the answer particularly mattered. Not now.

He shrugged. "Do we have to put a time limit on it? Why don't we just see how it goes?" His hard arm was warm around her back and his fingers caressed her waist and the curve of her hip. "Just think how good it will be for you. You won't have to find a new place to rent. You won't have to work extra jobs. You can build up your millinery business while we're together." When she would have risen, he held her in place. "If it's capital you're worrying about, I'll give you the money. How much do you estimate you'd need?"

She recoiled. Pain punched a hole through her heart. "I don't want your money."

"All right, if you won't accept a gift, I'll make it a low-interest loan. You can pay me back—we'll set up a monthly schedule."

"No." Quietly, but with steely resolve, she disentangled herself from his arms and rose, putting a safe distance between them. Her chest ached and the lump in her throat made it hard to speak. She swallowed. "Why are you so determined always to think the worst of me? Millions of people have had a bad experience with love and they don't use it as a shield to hide behind."

"I'm not hiding behind anything," he retorted, his eyes narrowing as the set expression on her face finally registered. "But I'm realistic. We enjoy each other's company. We like some of the same things. We're one hell of a match in bed." He stopped and looked away, his features hardening. "Love has nothing to do with what's between you and me."

The shattered shards of her heart were crushed to dust beneath the flat pronouncement. She studied him silently for a long moment, long enough that his gaze met hers again. He began to look distinctly uncomfortable under her uncompromising gaze. "If you truly believe that," she told him, "I feel sorry for you, Garrett. Sorry that you let your father's behavior and one woman's deceit dictate your entire future. Sorry that because of those bad breaks you're willing to throw away what we could have had together." She paused and walked to the doorway. "You're giving the past far too much power."

"I'm not—" His voice was tight, strident.

"I loved you," she said quietly. Tears were rolling down her cheeks but when he made an involuntary movement toward her she threw out a hand to stop him. If he touched her again, she'd break down completely. "My mother and father lost their chance at happiness but I was sure I'd found mine." She closed her eyes. "What a blind fool I was."

Silently she turned away then, walking down the hall and to the door. She didn't know where she was going but she knew she needed distance between them.

Garrett stood where she left him, his whole body rigid with denial. He heard the screen door open and close and her footsteps crossed the porch. Then he couldn't hear her anymore.

Finally he couldn't take the silence. He slammed the kitchen door behind him with a satisfying bang but the harsh sound did little to assuage the rage that boiled and churned inside him. His stomach hurt and his hands shook. His chest felt like it was banded with a restricting bar of iron. His thoughts whirled like a tornado, fragments rushing by too quickly for him to hang on to, torn away by the force of the gale.

Why would she lie to him like that? Surely she wasn't crazy enough to think he'd buy such an outrageous story. He swallowed repeatedly, but the lump in his throat wouldn't budge. Disappointment mushroomed, filling every corner of his being.

How could he have been so wrong about her? She'd seemed so different. But in the end, she wanted him for her personal gain, just as Kammy had. The only question now was how long she'd keep up the pretense of being wounded before she tried to get him to support her as he'd offered.

And she was wrong about him, he assured himself. The past didn't enter into this equation, except for its role in making him smarter and less gullible. His father had been a jerk, but that had nothing to do with today. *Nothing.*

He walked out onto the deck, noting that Ana was sitting on the edge of the dock, her feet dangling in the water. Abruptly he turned away, heading for the hiking trail that led around the lake. Angrily he kicked at sticks and pebbles as he strode along the path, then he veered away from the trail and began to hike through less accessible terrain. The physical challenge as he hiked over and around boulders and downed trees expended the worst of his first furious reaction, and a bone-deep sadness seeped in, chilling him despite his exertion.

Why? Why had she told him that?

Robin's heir would be entitled to a sizable portion of his estate, whispered an insidious little voice in his head.

Exactly. When she'd begun to speak, he'd felt his heart sink to his toes, leaving a leaden heaviness behind. Hadn't he told her he'd take care of her needs? Apparently that wasn't enough. She'd wanted more. A lot more.

Then an equally insistent thought intruded. *You could be wrong. Maybe she was telling the truth.*

Nah. He rejected it immediately. Of course she

wasn't Robin's daughter. Robin would have told him about that.

Wouldn't he?

For the first time in years, a tremor of insecurity rocked the stable world his stepfather had given him. *I'll introduce you to her soon. I believe you'll like her.* There hadn't been any hint of a leer, though Robin was too much of a gentleman for that anyway. But the quiet happiness that had shone from his still-vivid blue eyes had been unmistakable. He'd cared deeply for her. And back when Garrett assumed that Robin's ladylove was a dignified widow, he'd had no problem with it.

The problem had occurred when he'd met her and wanted her for himself.

Garrett stopped dead in the path. Slowly he lowered himself onto a rotting log and sat with his elbows on his knees, hands dangling between his knees while his breathing leveled out.

Good God. Was this all about jealousy? He was uncomfortably afraid that was exactly what had transpired.

How would he have felt if the older woman of his imaginings had inherited half the cottage? He forced himself to examine the scenario honestly. He would have been annoyed. More than annoyed. But would he have treated her as he'd treated Ana?

Absolutely, positively not.

An older woman, though, wouldn't be claiming to be Robin's biological daughter, he reminded himself.

He sat for a long, long time, watching the sun-dappled patterns of light and shadows play over the path and the edge of the lake where the trees grew right down to the rocks. Finally, as the shadows lengthened, he rose and started back toward the cottage.

It was a good thing the month had come to an end, he told himself firmly. He and Ana would only have one more uncomfortable night to get through before they headed back to Baltimore in the morning. He lifted a hand and pressed two fingers to his chest to relieve the pressure that centered there. Indigestion. That's all it was.

They wouldn't be spending that last night together.

He plodded on. As the cottage came into view between the trees, regret rose too large to suppress. The thing was, he could have been happy with Ana. She was comfortable to be with. He'd known enough women to know how rare it was to find someone with whom a shared silence wasn't a strain. In bed, he'd never known a woman so generous with herself, so able to rouse him to passion, so desirable. They both enjoyed the leisurely pace of life at the cottage, and he was certain she'd prefer a quiet lifestyle to a whirlwind trip to a high-rolling place like Las Vegas, as he did. She was a good cook, a quick wit, so tenderhearted that he longed to make the world perfect so that her heart would never be broken—

His feet stilled again. An inexorable tide of dread rose within him as he finally stopped lying to himself and faced the truth. He'd done exactly that—broken Ana's heart.

And his own, as well. The truth slapped him in the face.

Yes, he'd been jealous of Robin's relationship with her…because he'd wanted her for himself from the very first time he'd seen her. But even more, he'd begun to fall in love with her as he'd come to know her. *He loved Ana.*

In a single white-hot instant of clarity, he realized how little meaning his life would have without her. He could imagine waking to the sight of her glowing face each morning. He could imagine sharing the ups and downs of business and daily life with her. He could even, he realized with a sense of amazement, imagine adding a couple of kids to their lives: little girls with their mother's wild curls.

But the images froze as he recalled the devastation in her face before she'd walked away from him. He'd hurt her deeply, for reasons that now seemed petty and invalid. How could he make her understand that no matter how they'd first come together, he wanted to be with her forever?

A hint of panic touched his heart and he began to run up the path toward the cottage. He had a strong prescience of disaster, foreboding. He had to talk to Ana right away.

Inside he rushed up the stairs but she wasn't in her room. The door stood open, the room was empty. Not empty as in without a body, but unoccupied. Everything of any personal meaning gone.

A tiny demon of fear danced inside his gut as he forced himself to enter her studio. Also deserted. The counters were pristine and uncluttered again, the big worktable untouched. His gaze shot to the window beneath which she'd set her sewing machine, but the spot was as blank as it had been the day they'd arrived.

His lungs burned, and he realized he'd been holding his breath. Releasing it, he took a burning gasp of air. Ana was gone.

Nine

Ana was gone.

Her little car was no longer parked beneath the birches. Slowly Garrett moved down the stairs, confirming her flight with each step. Her beach towels no longer fluttered from the rail of the deck in the gentle breeze. The cat's bowl no longer occupied its place in the corner.

He stood in the middle of the kitchen, big hands lax at his sides. She'd left, and he really couldn't blame her. He'd been brutal. Moving into his office, he sat down in front of his computer, dashing off a quick request to his office manager in Baltimore to let him know when Ana Birch returned home, no matter how late it was, or how early tomorrow. He'd have to go after her and apologize.

He glanced up from the computer at the sketch of

Robin that had hung on the wall for years, since the office had originally been Robin's. It was one of his favorite images of Robin, clad in a casual sweater and pants. He sat on a rock by the lake in three-quarter view, a coffee cup cradled in both hands. A slight smile curved his lips, his eyes gazed into the distance. Garrett had seen him sit in that very pose more times than he could count.

"Well, old man, what do I do now?" he asked rhetorically, feeling the weight of hopelessness descend upon his soul. "You were right when you said I'd like her."

He stood and moved restlessly to the window. Something was bothering him, though he couldn't put his finger on it. Something...

Suddenly he snapped his fingers. Turning, he looked again at the picture of his stepfather. He'd never realized it before, but the picture had to have been drawn here, by a skilled artist who knew Robin well enough to capture that sweetly absorbed expression he often wore.

The hair on the back of his neck rose in automatic reflex as the truth kicked him in the face. *Ana's mother had drawn this.*

Walking across the room, his eyes scanned the bottom portion of the sketch—there. There, in the bottom left-hand corner: *JB.* And the date, all in a miniscule, elaborate cursive that looked as if she'd been drilled in the Palmer Method as a young girl.

Slowly he groped his way back to his desk without taking his eyes from the sketch. Sagging into his chair, he tilted his face toward the ceiling, closing his eyes as he exhaled heavily. An unyielding fist squeezed his chest, making it hard to breathe. He hadn't wanted to believe her but deep down, he'd known she wasn't lying.

And the proof hung right over there on the wall. Ana had told him her mother had gone through a brief pen and pencil phase before moving on to oils early in her career. Robin and Janette Birch had come here together, indeed, had created the cottage with their mutual needs in mind. And Ana's mother had sketched her lover in the setting where they'd been happy. No wonder Robin seemed to leap off the pa-per—Janette Birch had known him so well she probably could have drawn it without even having him in front of her. Just as Ana had drawn *him.*

Ana should have told him right away—but as he remembered his behavior in Baltimore, he knew he'd brought this on himself. No wonder she hadn't told him. He'd barely given her a chance. And she'd prob-ably realized early on that he'd call her a liar when she tried to explain.

He dropped his head into his hands and speared his fingers through his hair, tugging hard enough to make himself wince. He'd been utterly, completely despi-cable to her. Smug, condescending, superior. God, how would he ever get her to forgive him?

Abruptly he spun on his heel and headed for the stairs to pack. He needed to get back to Baltimore. But halfway there, he stopped abruptly. Her friends!

Ana wouldn't leave Maine without saying goodbye to her friends. He might have made some monumental misjudgments where Ana was concerned, but he knew how she felt about friendship. She'd never take off without talking to Teddy and his wife first.

Grabbing his car keys, he made one brief stop in the study before racing up the path to his truck.

It was a good thing cops in rural Maine were few and far between, he decided, or he'd have been nailed for exceeding the speed limit ten times over in his rush to get to town. When he pulled onto Main Street and saw the familiar little car parked in front of the art supply store, a wave of intense relief swamped him. He pulled into a parking space and simply sat for a moment, dropping his head forward to rest against his hands atop the steering wheel.

Thank God he'd caught her.

He straightened and began to climb out of the car. The momentary rush had faded and his steps felt leaden and hesitant. What could he say to her to fix the mess he'd made of things between them?

He was almost at the front door of the art supply shop when he saw Ana walking toward the door. His gaze met hers through the glass and she stopped for an instant, then slowly began to exit the store.

She forestalled him by asking, "Did I forget something?"

"No." How was he going to change her mind?

They stood there awkwardly for a long moment. Finally she took a wide step that would allow her to pass him.

"Ana, I don't want you to leave." He turned as she moved past him and walked with her toward the cars.

She shook her head without looking at him. "I

have to," she whispered. "Please don't, Garrett." Her car was parked in front of his larger vehicle and she wrenched the door open, fumbling for her keys. "You can have the cottage," she said. "When I get back, I'll go to Mr. Marrow's office and sign anything he needs to make you the sole owner."

"I don't want it," he said. "I want you. If you won't share it with me, I'll sell it."

Shock snapped her head up. "You wouldn't do that. Robin wanted you to have it."

"Your father wanted *us* to have it," he said.

"He—" Then his words sank in. "My father...?"

"I didn't want to believe you," he said. "I was jealous. Robin was *my* father in all the ways that mattered, and I couldn't stand the thought of someone else meaning more to him."

"Robin loved you so much," she said quietly. "No one could ever have taken your place in his life."

"I know that now," he said. "I'm sorry for all the things I said to you." His voice lowered. "The things I believed."

"Thank you." She appeared to have trouble getting the words out and she made a show of looking at her watch. "I have to go now."

But as she moved to slide into her car, Garrett caught her wrist. "I love you."

She stopped. "What?"

He slid to one knee, still holding her wrist, and he brought it to his mouth as he spoke again. "Ana, I love you. I want to marry you."

"Stand up," she said in a low voice, "and stop it. We're on Main Street!"

"I don't care." He didn't move.

Wildly she glanced around. Down the street, he could see a few tourists turning and staring. A man came out of the post office, glanced their way, and then stopped for a second look.

She tried to tug her hand free. "Garrett—"

"Marry me," he said again.

A bell trilled and he saw that Teddy had come out of his shop. "Everything okay?" her friend asked.

"Yes—"

"No," Garrett said. "I love her and I want to marry her. She hasn't said yes yet."

"Maybe that's because she doesn't feel the same way," Teddy said in a cool voice.

A sudden spear of uncertainty shot through him. "You said you loved me." But there was a hint of vulnerability in his tone and his grip on her wrist lessened.

A tear rolled down her cheek and she swiped at it with her free hand. "I do," she managed to say.

He stood and pulled her into his arms, folding her small body against him with all the tenderness he was feeling. "I don't want to wake up without you beside me," he said. "I don't want to spend a day wondering where you might be or if you've thought of me. I don't want to be like Robin, missing the only woman I'll ever love until the day I die." He ran his hands up and down her back. "I love you," he said again.

She swallowed. "It's not just sex?"

A chuckle from Teddy made them both stop and look his way. "A man doesn't chase a woman down Main Street and declare his love in front of half the town just for sex," he said, grinning. "I think he means it."

"I'll shout it loud enough for every one of them to hear if you want me to," he told her.

"No," she said hastily.

"Then say yes." He pressed a kiss to her forehead, overcome with the need to make her see how much he needed her.

"Yes." Her voice was a whisper.

Relief nearly made his knees buckle. "You'll marry me?"

"Yes," she said again. She pulled back enough to see his face, and a dawning radiance broke through the sadness that had shrouded her features. "Yes!"

"All right!" said Teddy.

Garrett barely heard him. All his attention was focused on Ana as he hauled her off her feet and swung her in a wide circle on the sidewalk. Clapping and laughter erupted from the people along the street. Her arms wound around his neck and he held her closely against him as he halted, searching for her mouth and kissing her deeply.

"I love you," he said. "And you're marrying me. Anything else is negotiable."

"Children?" she asked in a hopeful tone.

"As long as they don't come in pairs like his." He jerked his head in Teddy's direction. Then the import of their words hit him. "Grandchildren," he murmured. "Our children will be Robin's grandchildren."

Ana's eyes were bright with tears, but she was

smiling. "Nothing would have made him happier." Then she shook her head. "That old matchmaker."

"Matchmaker? More like manipulator," Garrett said, chuckling. "He knew I wouldn't be able to resist you any more than he could have your mother." He drew her close for another kiss. "Let's go home and make wedding plans."

"All right." She trailed a finger over his lips and his blood heated at the look in her eyes. "Let's go home."

* * * * *

Silhouette Desire

presents

DYNASTIES: THE CONNELLYS

A brand-new miniseries about the Connellys of Chicago,
a wealthy, powerful American family tied by blood to the
royal family of the island kingdom of Altaria.
They're wealthy, powerful and rocked by
scandal, betrayal...and passion!

Look for a whole year of glamorous and
utterly romantic tales in 2002:

January: **TALL, DARK & ROYAL** by Leanne Banks

February: **MATERNALLY YOURS** by Kathie DeNosky

March: **THE SHEIKH TAKES A BRIDE** by Caroline Cross

April: **THE SEAL'S SURRENDER** by Maureen Child

May: **PLAIN JANE & DOCTOR DAD** by Kate Little

June: **AND THE WINNER GETS...MARRIED!** by Metsy Hingle

July: **THE ROYAL & THE RUNAWAY BRIDE** by Kathryn Jensen

August: **HIS E-MAIL ORDER WIFE** by Kristi Gold

September: **THE SECRET BABY BOND** by Cindy Gerard

October: **CINDERELLA'S CONVENIENT HUSBAND**
by Katherine Garbera

November: **EXPECTING...AND IN DANGER** by Eileen Wilks

December: **CHEROKEE MARRIAGE DARE**
by Sheri WhiteFeather

Silhouette®
Where love comes alive™

Visit Silhouette at www.eHarlequin.com

SDDYN02